WEDDING BELL BLUES

KAYLEE

BOOK 2

JEFF
GOTTESFELD

STRIPPED

Stripped
Wedding Bell Blues
Independence Day
Showdown on the Strip

www.sdlback.com

Copyright ©2014 by Saddleback Educational Publishing
All rights reserved. No part of this book may be reproduced in any form or by any means, electronic or mechanical, including photocopying, recording, scanning, or by any information storage and retrieval system, without the written permission of the publisher. SADDLEBACK EDUCATIONAL PUBLISHING and any associated logos are trademarks and/or registered trademarks of Saddleback Educational Publishing.

ISBN-13: 978-1-62250-769-6
ISBN-10: 1-62250-769-X
eBook: 978-1-61247-980-4

Printed in Guangzhou, China
NOR/0914/CA21401458

18 17 16 15 14   2 3 4 5 6

For Emma, Impressive #1.

MEET THE CHARACTERS

ALANA: Heiress Alana Skye, daughter of famous billionaire hotelier Steve Skye, is drop-dead gorgeous. But her life has been less than happy. And she has a difficult time living up to her father's demand for perfection.

CHALICE: Rich girl Chalice Walker is one of Alana's besties. Her ditzy, fun-loving nature masks an old soul. College is not for her because she's an artist at heart.

CORY: In the glitzy world of Vegas, Cory Philanopoulos was Alana's rock. Then he went to Stanford and everything changed. Back for the summer, rekindling a romance with Alana is not on his radar.

ELLISON: Why is Ellison Edwards working as a personal trainer in the luxurious LV Skye Hotel when he can afford any Ivy League school? And he has the brains to get accepted.

KAYLEE: No stranger to poverty and hardship, Kaylee Ryan literally falls into her dream job at the LV Skye. As Alana Skye's personal assistant, no less. Will poor girl Kaylee get along with Alana's rich besties?

REAVIS: From Texas like Kaylee, Reavis Smith is determined to make it big in Sin City. He's a street magician with a secret identity. And he's making a name for himself all over town.

ROXANNE: Supermodel Roxanne Hunter-Gibson is beauty and brains combined. She's managed to make a killing with an entrepreneurial start-up. Now she's Steve Skye's latest hot squeeze.

STEVE: Self-made man, cunning, rude (and some would say a lot worse) are some of the words used to describe hotel billionaire Steve Skye. And his crowning achievement is the luxurious LV Skye Hotel and Casino on the Las Vegas Strip.

ZOEY: Zoey Gold-Blum is the hottest rich girl in town. She knows it. And she uses it to her advantage. Deferring college for a year, she is out to keep her besties Chalice and Alana all to herself.

CHAPTER ONE

Good morning, Kaylee. Room service!"

Kaylee Ryan was already awake when the knock came on the door of room 3121 on the thirty-first floor of the LV Skye Hotel in the heart of the Las Vegas Strip. She'd put in her order for 7:15 a.m. but set her alarm for 7:10 a.m. so she'd have time to use the bathroom and splash cold water on her face before breakfast arrived. The five-stars-plus LV Skye prided itself on being the most luxurious hotel in Vegas, where every detail mattered and where service was key. If a guest put in a breakfast room service order for 7:15 a.m., it was delivered not a minute later.

"Coming!" Kaylee called. She'd been at the window, gazing at an early June morning in Sin City, watching joggers, walkers, and passersby on the Vegas sidewalks.

She'd slept in shorts and a pink camisole she'd bought at Target. She still wore those things as she crossed the floor of a room that normally went for more than three bills a night.

Kaylee, though, was not paying a dime. That fact still felt impossible to her. Three weeks before, she'd arrived in Las Vegas an eighteen-year-old girl who was essentially homeless. Her first Vegas digs had been tacky room 109 at the zero stars Apache Motel, for which she paid one hundred and forty dollars. Not for a night. For a week.

She opened her hotel door and grinned. "Hey, Jamila," she told the African American server, who wore the crisp uniform of the kitchen delivery staff and carried Kaylee's breakfast on a tray. Behind Jamila was a silver cart with more room service orders. Kaylee and Jamila had met at the Apache. Kaylee was the reason that Jamila had this job.

"Morning yourself," Jamila told her. "Got your order. Carafe of high-octane coffee, two eggs over easy, hash browns, turkey sausage, and rye toast, no butter. Plus a glass of water. Gotta keep the executive assistant to Alana Skye fed and watered. Lemme bring it in, I've got a bunch more deliveries. And thank you again for this gig."

"Hey, it's the least I could do," Kaylee said happily. "Come on in."

When Kaylee had first met Jamila and her boyfriend, Greg, she'd been homeless, unemployed, and had her heart broken by a boy who she thought might become her first real boyfriend. Before she came to Las Vegas, she'd been sharing a derelict studio with her meth-head aunt Karen in the somewhat sketchy Echo Park section of Los Angeles.

She'd returned home from getting fired to find the apartment padlocked, their meager belongings in the driveway, and her aunt nowhere to be found. They'd been evicted; her aunt reportedly had taken off for San Francisco. Kaylee found herself on the street at four thirty in the morning. She'd gone to her "boyfriend" Victor's place only to find him counting money with a bunch of gangbangers. That was the end of their relationship before it really started.

There was nothing holding her in Los Angeles, so she'd come to Vegas in search of a new start—a blonde girl raised poor in Texas with not even a high school diploma to her credit.

Through the strangest series of events that she felt was either the hand of God or the best run of dumb luck in Vegas history, she found herself befriended by, and then working for Alana Skye. Alana, who was also eighteen, had the same last name as the LV Skye for a good reason. Her father, Steve Skye, was the hotel's owner, as well as the owner of dozens of other hospitality properties around the world. Alana ran Teen Tower, the LV Skye's special teen entertainment area. Within days of meeting her, Kaylee had been hired as Alana's assistant.

This luxury room was part of her pay. It was gold-on-white with blue accents, with floor-to-ceiling windows, a king-size bed, thick carpet, modern art on the walls, a flat screen TV, and a bathroom with tub, shower, bidet, and dressing area. It was five times the size of the shabby cubbyhole she'd rented at the Apache and about five hundred times as nice.

Jamila placed the tray on Kaylee's table. Then the girls embraced. "It's crazy you're living here, you know," Jamila told her.

"I think that every day," Kaylee responded.

"Well, Greg and I are just grateful you got us gigs."

Kaylee poured herself some of the hotel kitchen's high-end Indonesian coffee and took a grateful sip. She'd been up late the night before, going over Teen Tower plans with Alana in the luxury penthouse that her boss shared with her dad and her dad's latest gorgeous young girlfriend, Roxanne Hunter-Gibson.

"Hey. You would've done the same for me," Kaylee told her. "No doubt."

She took the room service ticket and signed it, adding a hefty tip for Jamila. She didn't have to pay for breakfast, but gratuities came out of her own pocket. It was great to be able to throw some money to her friend like this.

"What's up for you today?" Jamila asked.

"The usual," Kaylee reported. "Morning meeting with Alana. Then Teen Tower opens at ten. We're still getting four thousand kids a day. It's a money machine."

"Who's playing today?"

"Some band called ZZ Top. Steve asked for them specifically."

"Whoa. They're old! When was their last hit?"

"What Steve Skye wants, Steve Skye gets," Kaylee declared. "I think he wants to strap on a guitar and jam."

In addition to its pool, game room, no-money casino, gym, and all-you-can-eat dining room and food court, Teen Tower featured a daily three o'clock concert that was broadcast live on MTV. That had been Kaylee's idea. Though Teen Tower had only been open for a couple of weeks, the half-hour broadcast was already a national hit.

"Well, get me an autograph," Jamila said. "I'll send it to my grandfather."

Kaylee grinned. "Come by at two thirty. I'll introduce you."

Jamila put the signed check in her rear pocket. "You busy tomorrow night? Maybe you and one of those guys hanging all over you wants to go out with Greg and me."

Kaylee blushed. "There are not guys hanging all over me."

"Oh, please. I see how that dude in the gym wants to be with you. What's his name? Ellison, right? And your magic man Reavis? You told me he kissed you."

"Not so much lately," Kaylee corrected. "Reavis is working on his act, and Ellison—well, I'm not sure what he's been up to."

Reavis was Reavis Smith, an extremely talented magician and escape artist whom Kaylee had met at the Apache when he'd taken the room next to hers. He performed in a mask and called himself Phantom. She sometimes helped him with his tricks. His goal was to get a theater of his own and be bigger than Criss Angel. Reavis was street smart, as opposed to Ellison, who worked at the Teen Tower gym. Ellison was book smart in a way that Kaylee didn't think she could ever be. He was also tall, buff, and gorgeous. The main reason that he worked as a trainer instead of attending a top college like Harvard was to irritate his university professor parents.

Ellison had been interested in her for sure. He'd kissed her by surprise at the Teen Tower opening two weeks before. But since that time, nothing. In fact, he hadn't acted anything more than friendly. Not that Kaylee much minded. In so many ways, Ellison was out of her league.

Jamila checked her clipboard. "Okay. Schedule to keep. I gotta run. I'll text you. And don't worry about those dudes. There's ten more where they came from. You da bomb, girl."

They hugged one more time, and Jamila took off. Kaylee moved the breakfast tray to the table by the window, got out her laptop and phone, and went to work while she ate. Her first order of business was to read the *Stripped* blog. The blog was written by the two moms of Alana's bestie, Zoey Gold-Blum.

Stripped had all the latest news, gossip, celebrity spotting, and inside dirt on what was going on in town. At one point, Zoey's moms had threatened to do an exposé on Kaylee and her unsavory past. However, after the sensational Teen Tower opening that Kaylee had helped to engineer, complete with a surprise performance by Reavis behind his Phantom mask, the moms backed away from that idea. The moms could make or break anyone or anything in Vegas. Hotels, restaurants, performers, and people. They had that much power.

That morning, the blog was non-threatening, at least not threatening to Kaylee, Alana, Teen Tower, and the LV Skye. There was a nice review of Garth Brooks's new show at the Wynn. A chop job on a new restaurant near Caesars Palace that would put the restaurant out of business. An interview with the famed painter Jeff Koons, who was artist in residence at the LV Skye's Mondrian ultra-high-end restaurant—a restaurant that featured not just priceless modern art but also a working artist's studio. Some chatter about an upcoming charity event run by a group of trophy wives. Finally, Kaylee scrolled down to a gossipy piece about Alana's father, Steve, and his girlfriend, Roxanne:

> Our sources tell us that Steve Skye's been spotted at Harry Winston Jewelers in Los Angeles, as well as at a certain diamond dealer on New York City's Forty-Seventh Street. Not to go out on a limb and make a prediction, but *Stripped* isn't *not* making a prediction either. Since his divorce from troubled model Carli Warshaw, we've counted eleven girlfriends for the town's hottest bachelor. Who knows? Maybe Roxanne is going to be the last one.
> Good luck, Roxanne. You'll need it.

Huh. That was interesting. Kaylee wondered what Alana would think when she read it. Steve and Roxanne had only been together for a few months. Roxanne was only in her twenties. Not all that much older than Alana or Kaylee. What would it feel like for Alana to have—

Kaylee's cell rang. This was no shocker. As Alana's assistant, Kaylee's cell rang all the time. She answered without checking caller ID, assuming it was her boss.

"Morning, Alana," she said. "Did you read *Stripped* yet? Because there's this story about your dad—"

"Kaylee! Hi! Hi, love! How are you? Kaylee! It's me!"

Kaylee's heart pumped faster; she felt herself in the wash of an adrenaline flood. The coffee and food in her stomach turned over, and then over again.

It wasn't Alana on the phone at all. Instead, it was a female voice she dreaded hearing more than any other.

"Kaylee? You there, Kaylee?"

She hesitated a moment before responding. "Yes, Aunt Karen. I'm here."

She hadn't spoken a word to Karen since the night of the eviction. She didn't miss her. In fact, now that she had this great new job, she was glad that her aunt was out of her life, doing whatever she was doing in Northern California. Probably shooting meth, Kaylee thought.

"Wonderful! Fabulous! Terrific! Nothing better! It's *so* great to hear your voice!"

"Are you okay, Aunt Karen? How's San Francisco?"

"San Francisco? San Francisco?" Aunt Karen cackled a laugh roughened by a lifetime of booze, cigarettes, and meth. "What are you talking about, San Francisco? I'm not in San Francisco. I'm on the road! Guess who's comin' to Vegas? Me!"

Oh no. Aunt Karen was coming to town. That was a problem. No. That was a huge, giant, massive, enormous, gargantuan, colossal problem. As Karen prattled on, Kaylee solved a word problem in her head. The equation proved maddeningly simple:

Aunt Karen + Las Vegas + Kaylee = TROUBLE

CHAPTER TWO

A couple of hours later Kaylee was at work in the small office on the second floor of the Teen Tower complex that she and Alana had carved out as their workspace. It was nothing special—a couple of desks, computers, printers, filing cabinets, phones, and the like. Floor-to-ceiling one-way glass covered one of the walls so they could look down on the Teen Tower pool deck while they themselves were hidden from any guests' prying eyes.

The only special feature they'd installed were the security monitors that gave them simultaneous real-time views of all the Teen Tower recreation areas. The gym was on Camera 1, no-money casino on Camera 2, entry and security area on Camera 3, dining room on Camera 4, and so on. At this hour most of the activity was at the entrance, where kids waited patiently to be admitted. In the two weeks that Teen Tower had been open, they'd never had less than 3,700 paying customers on any one day.

Kaylee's first order of business was to check and double-check the arrangements for ZZ Top. The band had asked for several high school cheerleading and pompom squads to be their backup dancers. Since city schools were already out of session for the summer, Kaylee had to scramble the whole week to find cheer squads that would be willing to participate. It had taken many calls and e-mails, but she'd done it. Now those squads were going through their final dress rehearsal with the group at a band shell on the campus of the University of Nevada, Las Vegas. They'd be bused over to Teen Tower in the early afternoon. Kaylee was in charge of all the logistics. It was a bit of a nightmare.

She'd just come off the phone with the band's manager when Alana came sailing through the office door. She was dressed down in jeans, a regular Teen Tower T-shirt, and flip-flops. Her tawny dark hair framed a beautiful face with a cute nose, brown eyes, and flawless skin. "Hi, what are you up to?"

Kaylee resettled the phone handset on the receiver. "Just making sure things are together for the concert this afternoon."

"Are they?" Alana plopped down in the black leather chair by her desk.

"Totally."

Alana grinned. "Why am I not surprised? You're Miss Efficiency."

"I try to be, thanks." Kaylee swung her own rolling chair around toward her boss and friend.

"Good. What are you doing a week from Saturday?"

Kaylee shrugged. "Beats me. I'll be here, I guess. Why?"

"You won't be here," Alana intoned seriously. "I mean, you won't be at Teen Tower."

Well. That was a surprise. Kaylee wondered if maybe Alana was giving her the weekend off. She hadn't really had a day off, or taken a day off, since Teen Tower had opened. Maybe Alana was springing an Alana Skye-style treat and was going to fly Kaylee to New York. Or something.

Whatever Kaylee was thinking, she found out three seconds later that she was dead wrong.

"You're going to a wedding. I'm going to a wedding. We're all going to a wedding," Alana told her.

"Really? Whose?"

Kaylee had read the *Stripped* blog but couldn't believe that Alana was actually talking about Steve and Roxanne.

She thought that maybe the hotel was going to host a celebrity bash. Perhaps two of the many TV and movie stars who made the LV Skye their home away from Los Angeles and New York would be tying the knot.

Kaylee always found celebrity weddings slightly ridiculous. All that hoopla, and then she'd hear some months or years later that the couple was divorcing and "wished each other well." While they were wishing each other well, Kaylee wished that instead of their over-the-top nuptials, they would have donated the cost of their receptions and honeymoons to some worthy charity.

Alana leaned forward. "You read *Stripped* this morning?"

Well then. If she was talking about *Stripped*, it had to be—

"It's *true*?"

"It's true," Alana confirmed. "My dad. And Roxanne. And a couple thousand of their closest friends."

"They can't be getting married. They—they practically just met!" Kaylee yelped.

Kaylee knew the outlines of the backstory of Steve and Roxanne. Alana's father was divorced. Alana's mother, the former model Carli Warshaw, was currently a patient at a long-term care psychiatric facility in Georgia. In fact, she'd been there for a number of years. Alana had told Kaylee about Steve's post-Carli love life. He'd had a series of young, beautiful, and highly intelligent girlfriends since the divorce. Many of them weren't much older than Kaylee or Alana.

Roxanne Hunter-Gibson was the latest one of these model-intellectuals. Steve had even hired her to work alongside him at the hotel as a sort of informal personal assistant, the way that Kaylee was working for Alana. However, there was a big difference between Kaylee and Roxanne. Kaylee was not sleeping with her boss. And she most certainly was not marrying her boss.

Alana folded her arms and wrinkled her forehead. "Well, they're getting married anyway. They told me this morning. You and I are helping out with the wedding. Me more than you, I'd guess. In our copious free time," she added. "Get set for some long days and longer nights."

Kaylee stood and moved to the window that looked down on the pool deck, which was filling up with Teen Tower visitors. She saw short lines forming at the pool slides and plenty of swimmers. It was shaping up to be a Teen Tower day just like any other. "What do you think?"

"About them getting married?"

"Is there another topic?" Kaylee asked gently.

Alana laughed a little bitterly. "I guess not."

"So?"

Alana leaned back in her chair so that it tilted nearly to her desk; her lustrous dark hair falling down her back. "Well, I can say safely that what I think doesn't matter," she declared. "It was presented to me as a *fait accompli*. A done deal."

"But how do you feel?"

Alana laughed again. This time it wasn't a little bitter. It was a lot. "I'm not exactly jumping up and down at the idea of a stepmother who could be my sister. Roxanne kinda proved herself to be a first class bitch to me when we were starting up Teen Tower. You were here, you saw it. So forgive me if I'm not clamoring to be maid of honor. Not that they asked me."

Kaylee nodded. Nothing that Alana was saying wasn't true. Roxanne had been judgmental and difficult during the run-up to the Teen Tower opening. She tried to put herself in Alana's shoes and imagine Roxanne as a stepmother, inhabiting the same penthouse at the top of the LV Skye. It was a crazy concept to have a stepmother so young. The thought made Kaylee wonder if maybe Alana would be happier going far away to a good college.

"Well, maybe it will get canceled," Kaylee said, realizing even as she said it that this was not a particularly helpful comment.

Alana shook her head. "It'll happen. It's already in

Stripped. It'll be too embarrassing for my dad to back out now. Lucky me. Look. I guess it's between the two of them. I wish them all the luck in the world."

"I don't believe you," Kaylee said quietly. If she were Alana, she'd be hoping with everything she had that the wedding would get called off.

"I'm not asking you to." Alana took a deep breath and then changed the topic. "So, before we go down to work, what's going on in your love life? I haven't asked in a while."

"Love life? What love life?" Kaylee knew what was coming. She'd shared Reavis's secret identity with Alana. She had to. Reavis understood. And then she told her about the kiss right after Teen Tower opened.

Alana grinned a little. "Hey, Reavis and Ellison both kissed you at the Teen Tower opening. I think the only question to answer is whether you've kissed either of them back."

She then told Alana pretty much the same thing she'd shared with Jamila at breakfast. That is, how Reavis had been so distracted working on his magic act, and how Ellison had been more friendly than romantic. "I don't mind," Kaylee shared. "It lets me concentrate on work."

"I don't think you've ever told me what your longest relationship was?" Alana asked.

Kaylee bit the inside of her lip. "Well … I can't say I've ever really had one."

"What?" Alana exclaimed. "That's impossible."

Kaylee shook her head. "Not with me. You know how I grew up, and where I lived. It's not like Echo Park in Los Angeles is full of guys I was dying to date. Same thing with my grandmother's trailer park. There was a guy in the Echo who was about to be my boyfriend, but he turned out to be a gangbanger. No thank you."

"Well, I've liked some guys," Alana declared. "But I really like Cory. And I thought it was serious. If only he liked me back as much as I like him."

Cory was Cory Philanopoulos. Tall, rangy, sandy-haired; he'd been Alana's boyfriend when she was in eleventh grade, but they'd split up when he went away to Stanford. They'd recently started seeing each other again. But only as friends.

Alana had given Cory a Teen Tower job, working in the social media department. Kaylee had met Cory several times and liked him. He came from a lot of money but didn't act like it. Plus, he wasn't as intimidating as Ellison, who was so well-educated that Kaylee felt stupid in comparison. He'd read everything, played all kinds of musical instruments, and looked like an ebony god.

Cory was just as handsome, but a lot more humble. She

liked that. She could see why it was that Alana liked him so much. In another world, she could see herself liking him too. Not in this world, though. Not when her boss was all over him.

"You guys are going out a lot," Kaylee told her. "Right?"

Alana nodded. "Yeah. But it's like … friends. I don't just want to be friends with him."

"Don't rush it," Kaylee cautioned.

Alana's grin spread wide across her face. For the first time since she'd come into the office, she actually seemed to relax. "Why should I listen to you?" she asked. "You've never had a boyfriend!"

Kaylee laughed. Her friend had a point. "Okay, you're right. But still …" She got an idea. Maybe there was a way for her to help out Alana. "You know, I can maybe talk to him for you."

"You mean, like, we're still in middle school?" Alana scoffed.

"No. More to see, like, what he's thinking. And to say lots of nice things about you. I promise."

"Okay," Alana agreed. "But keep it cool." She stood and smoothed out the back of her T-shirt. "Anything else I need to know before we go down? Let's meet for lunch at one."

Kaylee hesitated. She knew she should tell Alana about the phone call she'd received from her crazy druggie aunt. When she'd been hired, she hadn't said anything about Aunt Karen; keeping the information a secret had almost cost her the job. At the same time, she didn't want to have to drag Alana into the mess of her screwed-up family life.

Karen had gushed about coming to Las Vegas from San Francisco. But Kaylee couldn't actually imagine her aunt showing up here. Where would she even get bus fare? It wasn't like she had a car of her own.

"You're not telling me something," Alana announced. "Bad idea."

"Am I really so obvious?"

Alana nodded. "Don't take up poker. Spill."

Kaylee talked about Aunt Karen, and how much the idea that Karen was now in Vegas concerned her. Alana listened. When Kaylee was done, Alana was reassuring.

"Don't worry about a thing," she told Kaylee. "She's not going to bother you."

"Don't hurt her."

Alana shook her head. "No one's hurting anyone. But if she shows up here, we've got your back. I'm glad you told me what's going on. Now let's get to work. We've got a Teen Tower to run."

Kaylee smiled, went to the office door, and opened it. "And a wedding to plan."

"Lucky us."

As they headed for the elevator to the main level, Kaylee wondered what a wedding reception involving Steve Skye would look like. As it turned out, her wildest imagination didn't begin to approach reality.

CHAPTER THREE

There were a lot of great things about being Alana's assistant at Teen Tower, but Kaylee's favorite was that it was part of her job just to wander around the big complex, taking in everything, making notes about things she didn't like or that needed fixing, and talking to the guests.

It had taken her a while to build the courage to approach a group of strangers and say, "Hi, I'm Kaylee Ryan. I'm on the executive staff here at Teen Tower. How's it going? Are you having a good experience?" But after two weeks, it was second nature. She didn't even bother with a notebook anymore. She just talked her notes into her smartphone to be played back later.

By late that same morning, Kaylee had already been through the Teen Tower dining area, the virtual reality game room, and the new Teen Tower makeover district, where visitors could have their hair and makeup done by a team of professionals. This had been Kaylee's idea; it had taken only forty-eight hours for it to be licensed, outfitted, and up and running. Such was the power of Steve Skye. The salon was proving so popular that kids were reserving appointments two, three, and four weeks in advance.

Kaylee had dictated several important notes before she went to her midday rendezvous with Alana out on the pool deck. She'd noticed that in the dining room, guests were chowing down on the homemade pistachio ice cream but not so much on the strawberry. They needed more pistachio, and they needed better strawberry. In the virtual reality game room, guests lined up for the MMA game, while motorcycle racing was ignored. Kaylee made a note to get two more mixed martial arts games. Then, as she headed toward her meeting with Alana, she noticed a few more things that should be addressed. She stopped to dictate a note.

As a result of the delay, Kaylee was a couple of minutes late to her midday meet up. As Kaylee threaded her way through the people enjoying themselves on the pool deck, she could see that Alana wasn't alone. She was with her best friend, Zoey.

Almost from the moment that Kaylee had met her,

Zoey had careened between an attitude of snobbish disdain and cold dislike. Alana had said that when Zoey was nice, she was a loyal friend whose fearlessness was inspiring. Kaylee had never seen her nice, though. The best she'd ever gotten out of Zoey was invisibility—Zoey sometimes acted like Kaylee didn't even exist.

Zoey was beautiful. Five foot eight, with short natural blonde hair, a pert thin nose, and simmering blue eyes. While Alana wore a beautiful paisley sundress and brown sandals, Zoey was dressed to thrill in the shortest blue cutoffs that Kaylee had ever seen and a white bikini top. To her shock, Zoey greeted her warmly as she approached. "Kaylee! Hey! How are you, girl? How's every little thing?"

Kaylee's defenses went to Code Red even as she responded in kind. "Good, Zoey. How are you?"

"I'm great," Zoey told her. "I'm loving my new job."

"Cool! Where are you working?" Kaylee was still trying to figure out what was going on here when Alana broke into the conversation.

"She's working right here," Alana explained. "Here at Teen Tower. She's starting off as a motivator hostess here at the pool. And then we'll see where it goes."

Huh. This was a surprise. Alana hadn't even hinted that Zoey was joining the Teen Tower staff. The motivator hostesses were the young women whose job it was to organize all the pool-deck activities. If there was to be a belly-flop contest, the motivators would run it. If there was to be water polo with a giant beach ball, they would divide the teams and keep the games going. They also ran dance contests, games, and raffles. They were the paid life of the party. It was the perfect gig for Zoey. When she wore cutoffs and a bikini top like the one she had on now, no guy would ever say no to her.

Kaylee let discretion be the better part of keeping her job, though the idea that loathsome Zoey would be around all the time made work less fun. "Welcome aboard."

"Chalice is gonna work here too," Alana added. "She's heading over to the makeover district to be the official photographer."

Chalice was Chalice Walker, Alana's other best friend in Vegas. She was short, red-haired, and dazzlingly curvy. She always seemed a step behind any conversation. Her father, though, was the most powerful lawyer in town and came from old money. All the casinos used him both as counsel and as a lobbyist in the state capital. Zoey and Alana both liked Chalice, though Kaylee couldn't figure out why. There had to be something. Anytime Kaylee had ever seen Chalice, Zoey was always a few feet away. She was like a redheaded remora to Zoey's great white shark.

Alana's iPhone rang; she checked the number. "My dad. I'm being summoned," she told Kaylee and Zoey. "I'll check with you later."

Without anything else, she stepped away to talk to her father.

"Surprised?" Zoey asked.

"By what?"

"By me working here," Zoey said, her voice sweet and artificial.

"Why should it bother me?" Even as she asked the question, she knew it wasn't honest. It was bothering her a lot. And it bothered her most of all that Alana hadn't talked about it with her beforehand.

"Because I think you have a plan," Zoey told her. "You're not just working with Alana, you're all buddy-buddy with her. She thinks you're the best thing since text messaging. I don't have a problem with you working here. I think you're good at it. But if you think you're going to turn my bestie against me, you're in for a big surprise."

Kaylee bristled. "I don't want to turn her against you."

Zoey started to back away. "Remember this conversation." Then she turned on her heels and headed for the far end of the pool deck.

Kaylee stood still, a bit stunned. Her personal rule when things were upsetting was to let them bother her for five minutes and then get on with her life. Sometimes it wasn't possible, but a lot of times it was. She gave herself five minutes of walking around the pool deck to settle, then continued with work. She stopped briefly in the gym where Ellison flashed a friendly smile but didn't break away from what he was doing to talk. Then she headed toward the social media room where Cory was keeping up the Teen Tower website, Instagram, Tumblr, and Twitter presence.

She didn't have to get that far, though. She practically ran into Cory outside the faux casino where he'd stopped for a break of his own.

"In a gambling mood?" he joked after they'd greeted each other.

Cory was the kind of guy who made girls' heads turn, and Kaylee was not immune. She noticed his intense blue eyes and the small cleft in his chin. He wore jeans, a black T-shirt, and simple flip-flops. She'd gotten to know him during the early days of Teen Tower. He'd actually been part of the plot with Reavis and Alana that got the magician to perform at the Teen Tower opening.

"In the mood to do my job," she retorted. Then she realized there might be a way for her to put her plan about talking to him on Alana's behalf into action, starting now. "Hey. Want to walk through the casino with me? Tell me if you see anything out of order? I could use some extra eyes."

He grinned. "Like a dealer pocketing chips? There's no money in this casino."

"You know what I mean," she faux-chided him. "Like there not being enough open tables for kids to play. Stuff like that."

"I'd love to. Let's do it."

The no-money casino was one of the most popular amusements at Teen Tower. Every guest admitted to Teen Tower was given a certain number of chips to gamble. Those chips could be wagered just like real money at poker tables, roulette wheels, blackjack tables, craps tables—just about every kind of casino game except for slot machines and video poker.

When Teen Tower was designed, Steve Skye decided not to put in electronic games, which he thought were isolating and solitary instead of being communal and fun. His instincts, as usual, had been on target. There were groups of kids at every table. The din of rock and roll played through the sound system. And the shouts and groans from the winners and losers were as noisy as in the adult casino next door, where tens of millions of real dollars were wagered every day.

Kaylee and Cory took separate paths around the kid

casino floor and then regrouped. Neither had anything to report that was out of the ordinary, which suited Kaylee just fine. She'd send in a good write-up to Steve, who might give the casino pit boss a raise.

Kaylee loved casinos. When she'd first come to Vegas, she'd thought the idea of gambling, whether the gambling was real or pretend, was stupid. A few turns at the Apache Motel slot machine showed how much she could enjoy it. It was illegal for people under twenty-one to gamble for real money, but she'd found a way. Once, she found herself playing for hours. It calmed her. Centered her in a way.

"It would be fun to come here with Alana sometime," Kaylee said.

"I'm not sure she's a big gambler."

"Hey, the Alana I know is up for anything!"

Cory smiled. "I imagine that's true. So, tell me. If Alana is up for anything, what are the kinds of things that Alana's trusted assistant is up for?"

Kaylee tried to steer the conversation back to her boss. "I'm up for whatever Alana says I'm up for. She's such a cool girl. Gorgeous. Smart, interesting … she took a big chance hiring me, you know."

Cory nodded. "I do know. Seems to have worked out well for both of you, I'd say."

"What do you think?" Kaylee pressed. "You think Alana might want to come here sometime after work with you, just to have fun? You should ask her."

Before Cory could answer, a nerdy kid with a friendly smile tapped him on the shoulder. "Hey, man, sorry to interrupt."

"We work here," Kaylee said to the kid. "It's no problem. How can we help you?"

The kid lowered his voice. "Well, I couldn't help overhearing that you were talking about maybe coming here on a date or something. I rep a place—it's not big or anything, very private, really—where you can gamble for real."

Kaylee raised her eyebrows. "For real? As in real money?"

The kid nodded. "Yep. Private place. Small. North of the freeway. In a warehouse. But we got all the games. Roulette, blackjack, like that. Set up like a club, so teens are fine. I'll put you on the list."

Her heart thumped. This kid was saying that there was a place where she could gamble without getting into any trouble. For real stakes.

Wow. She didn't hesitate. She didn't even check in with Cory about it. "You do that," she told the kid, taking the card he gave her with the address and putting it carefully into her back pocket. "Thanks, man. See you there soon."

"You know, Kaylee," Cory said firmly, "that kid shouldn't be passing out his card to Teen Tower guests. Their parents will freak."

"I'll have security keep an eye on him," Kaylee replied. Cory was right. They needed to stop the kid from giving out cards. But she was glad she got one of them before they did.

CHAPTER FOUR

It had been a rugged day, probably Kaylee's toughest one on the job since she'd started. First, there was the disturbing news about Aunt Karen. Then, there was the surprise about the wedding. And there was Zoey and Chalice joining the staff at Teen Tower. But that wasn't all. It got worse. Between the time that ZZ Top finished rehearsing and their arrival at the LV Skye, their drummer came down with what the doctors called "severe intestinal distress." Not only did Kaylee have to find another drummer to fill in for him, but she had less than two hours to do it.

In typical Kaylee fashion, she'd made it happen. She went online and learned that at the Vegas Dreams Hotel, a cheap downtown tourist destination, there was a nightly music tribute show where a group of performers did spot-on imitations of artists from Eminem to Rihanna to the Beatles to JLo. One of the songs in their repertoire was by ZZ Top. Kaylee tracked down the group's drummer, who turned out to be a ZZ Top fanatic. When Kaylee told him he could actually play with his idols if he got his butt to Teen Tower, the guy practically swooned on the phone. He showed up, got the charts for the songs, and the three o'clock show went off perfectly. When the drummer was introduced to the crowd and took his bow, Kaylee wondered if he'd float away with pride. Steve Skye strapped on a guitar to join in the encore song, "La Grange." To Kaylee's surprise, he didn't suck.

By the time Teen Tower closed that day, Kaylee felt like she'd earned a break. Fortunately, the break was there to take. In her pocket was the card the kid she and Cory had met in the no-money casino, plus a password that he said would be good for that night only. She could bring up to three friends. Kaylee knew who she wanted her guests to be: Alana and Cory. It would be the perfect time to try to get the two of them together. Cory agreed immediately. Alana wasn't a hard sell after Kaylee said that Cory would meet them there.

The underground casino was open between nine and midnight. It had a dress code, so Kaylee dressed nicely.

She was paid seven fifty a week at Teen Tower, but her room and food were free, so she had some money available to buy clothes. She'd discovered a consignment store on the other side of the freeway that specialized in designer clothes. At this resale shop, she had found three or four great outfits, including a sleek and clingy red dress by Versace, which Alana had immediately pronounced, "Hot to the max." She put that on for the night, plus red and black pumps. Then she did her makeup carefully, brushed out her hair, and met Alana down in the lobby.

Alana looked stunning in a gray cocktail dress she said was by Marchesa. They took one of the hotel limos to the club. It was Kaylee's first time in a limousine. She was wowed. The exterior was black, the interior black leather, and there was a fridge, TV, computer with Internet access, and a couch that folded down in case it was a long journey and the occupants wanted to sleep.

"This isn't even the nicest limo," Alana told her as the driver headed north into the same district where Kaylee had found her favorite resale shop. "My dad has his own. Made by Rolls-Royce especially for him."

"How much did it cost?" Kaylee asked.

"Whatever number you're thinking of, add some zeros," Alana responded.

Kaylee thought about that. She wondered how much

Alana and Cory might be gambling tonight. They had so much money. For them, betting a thousand dollars might be the same as Kaylee wagering ten dollars. Or maybe wagering ten thousand dollars would be the same as her wagering ten dollars. She tried to imagine what that felt like, to live in a world where money lost its value. Since Alana and Cory both came from that world and were comfortable there, it was another reason for them to be together. She decided that was something she could tell Cory.

"You looking forward to hanging with Cory?" Kaylee asked.

Alana nodded distractedly. "Yeah. I guess. You talked to him today, right?"

Kaylee nodded. "I said a lot of nice things about you."

"Well, let's hope they get through his thick skull," Alana told her as the limo driver slowed and pulled into a parking lot big enough to hold a few hundred cars. "I think we're here."

They had arrived. The limo stopped in front of what looked like a warehouse. A single beefy man stood in front of a steel door. Kaylee and Alana approached him. The man said nothing until Kaylee and Alana each offered the password that had been provided. "North Dakota."

The man nodded. "Welcome. Enjoy."

He opened the door. The girls stepped into a small version of a regular Vegas casino. There was a brief stop at an information desk where they filled out some paperwork and got membership cards that indicated they had entered a private club. "That's how they can get away with the gambling," Alana told Kaylee. "A club's a club. But they still need to be careful."

Kaylee looked around. The place was smaller than the no-money casino at Teen Tower, but there were table games, slot machines, and a no-alcohol bar. All the guests were young and well dressed. As at Teen Tower, most of the activity seemed to be around the table games. There was a big crowd at one of the craps tables where some guy seemed to be on a serious winning streak.

"You see Cory anywhere?" Kaylee asked.

Alana shook her head. "Let's look for him."

They started off toward the roulette section. They didn't get very far, though, before a familiar voice called to them from behind. It wasn't Cory. "Hey, hey! Alana and Kaylee? You're here? What a surprise. This is great!"

They turned. There was Ellison, looking buff and dapper in a gray suit over a black T-shirt. What a surprise to see him here. *Or maybe it shouldn't be such a surprise*, Kaylee thought. This place had to have been operating for a while, and Ellison had been in Vegas for a while. Maybe

Kaylee was the last one to know that this place existed. She wondered if Cory knew about it before. Maybe not. He'd been away at college after all.

"Ellison!" Alana exclaimed. "What are you doing here?"

"Hey, this is the place," he said a little slyly. "I like to come here and get my blackjack on. You girls look fly. Alana, you're always beautiful. Kaylee, you look great. When did you decide you like the action?"

"The action?" Kaylee asked.

"The action, gambling, wagering, all this," Ellison said, spreading out his arms. "What's your game?"

"Blackjack," Kaylee said to avoid embarrassment. It was the only casino game she thought she understood well enough not to make a fool of herself. That and roulette. But roulette was tough to win; the house had too big an advantage. Blackjack had more reasonable odds.

"Are you girls here alone?" Ellison asked.

Kaylee shook her head. "Cory was supposed to meet us here."

Ellison pointed toward the far end of the casino. "You know, I think I saw him back that way, toward the craps tables. Why don't I walk Alana over there so you can settle down and get warmed up? We'll catch up with you."

"That's a great idea," Alana agreed.

"Sounds good if that's what you want," Kaylee said.

For her, the plan was perfect. What she really wanted to do was settle down and gamble for some real money for the first time in her life. Playing the slot machines in the motel reception area had been okay, but it wasn't the same. That was a quarter at a time. Tonight, she had the chance to *really* play.

Alana and Ellison took off. Kaylee looked around for a blackjack table with an open seat. She found one quickly—it was actually just her and a female dealer. The minimum bet was only two dollars. She'd brought a hundred dollars with her, and turned it in to the dealer for fifty two-dollar chips. With a stack of red chips in front of her, she started to play. Two quick blackjacks with a five-chip bet on each turned the fifty chips into sixty-five in a hurry. She was elated. "Yes!"

"You're having good luck," the dealer said. She was small and efficient.

"I'll say," said a voice behind Kaylee.

She turned. There was Cory, looking elegant in a slacks and sweater combo. "Hey, Cory," she said to him. "Alana was looking for you."

He waved toward the far end of the casino. "Saw her. She's hanging with Ellison. They're playing craps. I said

I'd check up on you. So, I'm checking up. Mind if I play a while?"

"I'd love that."

Kaylee patted the stool next to her, and the dealer gave Cory a welcoming smile. He had a pocketful of chips already and started playing with gold five-dollar ones. He bet several of them on a hand where he could split a pair of twos into two hands. "I'm doing that because the dealer is showing a six. Odds are in my favor."

Cory was right. He won both hands. Kaylee, in the meantime, played cautiously, winning more than she lost. She felt wonderful. There was just something about watching her stack of chips grow that was fun, calming, exciting, and intoxicating all at the same time.

"You like this, huh?" Cory asked her.

Kaylee nodded. "Yeah."

Cory smiled. "It's better than drinking, in my humble opinion. No one ever got into an accident for driving while gambling."

Kaylee laughed. "I guess not." Then she remembered her mission of helping the Alana-and-Cory thing along. She had a job to do. "Don't you want to go play with Alana? It looks like you're everyone's good luck charm. You guys can play for big stakes together. You're so lucky. It's like you were born for each other."

"Nah. Never leave a table while you're winning. That's Las Vegas rule number two." He touched the stack of chips in front of him. "And I'm winning. So maybe it's you who's the good luck charm."

"What's rule number one?" Kaylee asked.

"Gamble next to a pretty girl," he declared.

She laughed. "Another reason for you to hang with Alana. Anyway, it's going to take a long time to get rich with two-dollar chips and with two-dollar minimum bets," Kaylee told him as she won yet another hand when the dealer busted. She did a quick count of her chips. She was up almost forty dollars.

"Just keep doing what you're doing," Cory counseled.

Kaylee did. She and Cory kept playing and joking around and winning. She had a great time. At some point, they saw Alana and Ellison walk up to a craps table together. They waved at Cory and her. She and Cory waved back. Kaylee hoped that they were winning too.

On the next hand, she bet a stack of five red chips. Ten dollars total. The dealer busted.

"Good girl!" Cory shouted and gave her a little hug.

"Do good girls gamble?" Kaylee asked him.

He smiled at her. "Goodness is highly overrated."

She pushed five chips forward onto the bet line for the next hand. "Well then," she told him. "Let the games begin."

CHAPTER FIVE

The morning after the visit to the secret casino, Kaylee was in a great mood. She'd had an excellent time. Not only had she come out a winner by a hundred and thirty dollars, but it had been fun hanging with Cory. She could see more than ever why Alana liked him so much. It was a little strange realizing that she and Cory had probably spent more time together at the casino than Alana and Cory had spent together. But Kaylee thought that in the long run it might be for the best. Every time she could, she said something nice about Alana to Cory.

    The next morning was normal. It had started with a meeting in Steve Skye's office to get into some of the early wedding planning. It was made clear right away to Kaylee that she need not be more than a helper in that process. The wedding itself would be put together by Steve, Roxanne, a wedding planner named Abra who'd been brought in from New York, and Alana.

Alana's friends Zoey and Chalice, because of family and business reasons, not to mention the *Stripped* blog, would also have a fair amount to do. Kaylee's main role would be to work extra hard at Teen Tower. At best, Kaylee might get called and asked to do some small wedding errands. That was it. She wasn't in the planning meeting for more than fifteen minutes. Alana and company, though, stayed for more than two hours.

Alana was back on the job at Teen Tower sampling fresh-pressed juices in the dining room when the call came for Kaylee.

It was the head of hotel security. "Kaylee? Charlie Alvarez here. Can you come to my office? There's someone here I think you need to see."

Oh no. Kaylee knew without asking who was there, but she asked anyway.

"Is Karen Clarke with you?"

"That's a big ol' affirmative," Charlie confirmed. "We've got her here. She keeps asking to see you."

Blech. She'd hoped Karen would detour en route to Vegas. When she hadn't heard from her for a day, she let the seed of that hope flower. This call officially yanked that mental pansy out by the roots. There was only one possible response.

"I'm on my way."

With a quick text to Alana, Kaylee announced where she was going. Alana said it was fine, and Kaylee made her way over to the LV Skye security office. By the time she got to the main hotel lobby, she'd broken out in a cold sweat at the anticipation of seeing her druggie aunt. At the same time, she realized that if Karen hadn't managed to get them evicted from the Echo Park studio, Kaylee never would have come to Vegas. If she hadn't come to Vegas, fate never would have brought her to where she was right now—Alana Skye's assistant, the best job any girl could ever want, with a free hotel room and a decent salary.

"Life is strange," Kaylee muttered to herself.

She made her way to the rear service entrance and took the elevator down three floors. The doors opened into the hotel security complex. The complex took up a whole sub-basement floor and was like a war room. More money went through the LV Skye in one day than most people could ever dream of, and so much of it was cash. With thousands of rooms and employees and tens of thousands of daily visitors drinking countless numbers of beers, bottles of wine, and mixed drinks, the odds of trouble were better than the odds of losing at a sucker game like Keno where the house had a thirty percent advantage. That is, it was just about a sure thing.

The hotel security chief, Charlie Alvarez, had been the chief of police in San Antonio, Texas, before Steve had hired him away. He was a stocky Latino whose Texas drawl belied the steel in his eyes and great intelligence.

"Hey there, Kaylee," he greeted her easily. Charlie still wore a Texas-style cowboy hat and tilted it up so he could see her better.

"Hi, Charlie. My aunt is here?"

"Indeed she is. We picked her up in the hotel lobby per Steve's orders."

Kaylee winced, remembering what Karen had looked like when they lived together in Echo Park. Nasty and smelly. Doing that twitchy thing that so many meth addicts did all the time.

"How is she?"

"Well, we didn't have to cuff her. Fact is, she was nice as could be. She's in room five. Come on, I'll walk you down."

Charlie started toward the holding area where security brought people before turning them over to the Vegas police. They also detained unruly folks until they sobered up. The holding rooms were actually pretty nice, with couches, chairs, and a wall-mounted TV, plus a small bathroom. On the other hand, they had no windows, and the doors could only be locked from the outside. Charlie put a fob against a sensor of one of the doors. It clicked open.

"Kaylee!"

Karen raced across the room and embraced her. To Kaylee's surprise, her aunt didn't smell bad or look drugged out. She'd cut her scraggly hair even shorter than Zoey's and wore clean jeans, a black men's work shirt, and tennis shoes. Her blue eyes were clearer than Kaylee remembered, and for the first time Kaylee could recall, she didn't reek of cigarettes. When Kaylee was a little girl and Karen had just come out to Hollywood to try her hand at acting, her aunt had been a genuine beauty. She was no beauty now, but at least she didn't need a high-pressure fire hose to get cleaned up.

"Hi, Karen." Kaylee disengaged from the embrace as quickly as she could. If Karen had fleas in her clothes or lice in her hair, she didn't want them jumping skin to skin.

Charlie cleared his throat. "Um, Kaylee? You'll need to escort her off-premises one way or the other," he said softly. "But you're welcome to stay here and visit as long as you want. Door's open. Check with me on your way out."

Kaylee nodded that she understood, and Charlie departed discreetly. Now it was just the two of them. Karen had heard full well what Charlie said. She had to leave. Still, like it or not, Karen was the one connection to her family that Kaylee had left, not counting her own father in prison.

"How are you, Karen?" she asked cautiously.

"I'm good, good," Karen said, her gravelly voice full of enthusiasm. "Was up in the Bay Area for a few weeks. Got myself clean up there, now I'm here. Hey, you're doing great. I hear you're doing great. One of my friends read about you on the Internet. You're working here? That's my niece! I knew you could do it!"

"So far, so good," Kaylee answered.

"Assistant to Alana Skye. That means money. Not that I want her money. No. Hey, I'm just glad to see you." Karen held her arms out wide, like she wanted another hug.

Kaylee didn't hug her but did hold her aunt's hands. "So, you're here in Vegas. What are your plans? You just passing through?"

"I don't know," Karen admitted. "I don't really have a place to stay or any plans. But this cool dude in San Francisco spotted me five hundred bucks, so I have a little money. And I'm clean. See?" She held out one of her hands. It trembled only slightly, which was far better than

Kaylee remembered from Los Angeles. "Maybe I'll find work and stick around. Who knows?"

"I'm sorry you can't stay with me," Kaylee declared. "They've got me in a room here at the hotel. No guests allowed."

Karen protested. "Hey! I'd never ask to stay with you. I'm ready to be my own person. I just need a little help, being new in town and all. You have any ideas where I could crash? Got any friends who could use a reliable roommate?"

Okay. That was unintentionally funny. After what had happened in Echo Park, the idea of Kaylee referring Karen to be anyone's "reliable" roommate was less likely than ten jackpots in a row on a slot machine. However, Kaylee was nothing if not practical. If she didn't help Karen find a place to stay, she knew Karen would return to hang around the LV Skye. There would be repeated visits down here to security, and Charlie Alvarez would get less and less patient with each ensuing one. No. There had to be a better way.

A moment later, Kaylee had it.

"Get your stuff, Karen," she told her aunt. "We're out of here."

An hour later, Kaylee was installing her aunt in room 109 of the Apache Motel out by UNLV. It was the exact same room where she'd stayed when she'd first come to town. She'd negotiated the exact same deal with the desk clerk, Al, that she'd had for her first seven nights in town: a hundred and forty a week. Karen had paid cash. Al had handed over the key and TV remote, no questions asked. Because it was Kaylee with her, Al hadn't even asked Karen for a credit card.

"You'll be safe here," Kaylee said as Karen entered and dropped her two shopping bags full of clothes on the threadbare bedspread.

"This isn't half bad," Karen said approvingly. "And there's a pool!"

"There's a diner down the street that has sandwiches, and Al will sell you frozen food for the microwave." Kaylee felt stressed as she gave her aunt the lay of the land. She'd borrowed one of the hotel's cars to drive over here—one of the Beamers—and wondered if she needed to vacuum it before she went back to work. What if Karen really did have lice? It was possible. Ugh. She had let Karen embrace her. What if *she* had lice now too? Wasn't that an itch she felt under her left arm? Argh!

"Anything else I need to know?"

Kaylee shook her head. "Nah. You're good here. I've got your number. Al at the desk is okay if you stay on his good side. I've got a buddy next door named Reavis. I'll tell him you're here. But only contact him if it's an emergency." She made a show of checking her cell. "I gotta go."

"When will I see you again?"

"Soon," Kaylee said noncommittally.

"Okay. See ya."

Kaylee left without any additional bodily contact. She was glad that Karen hadn't yet asked her to try to help her get a job at the LV Skye. But she was skeptical. Her instincts were good because her peace of mind didn't last a minute. Just as she was passing by the office, her cell sounded. It was an incoming text from Karen.

"Hey doll! U think u can help your aunt get work at that hotel of yours?"

Double argh. Kaylee didn't answer. She did, however, say hi to Reavis, who happened to be at the front desk paying his bill for the week to come. He was medium height, stocky without being fat, and had grown his sideburns long since Kaylee had seen him last. The greatest magician in Vegas, known only by the name Phantom, flashed a ready smile at Kaylee.

"Hey. Why the long face? And what you doing back here anyway? Get bounced from Steve Skyeland?"

"All good at Skyeland," Kaylee reported. "But the crazy aunt show has arrived."

"The one from L.A.? The druggie?"

"The druggie," Kaylee confirmed. "She seems clean now. She's in room 109. I told her she could knock on your door in an emergency. Or call your room. Or whatever." Kaylee shook her head darkly. It felt unkind, but she wished all over again that Karen hadn't showed up like this.

She looked over toward the two slot machines in the lobby. Like so many other motels, bars, and even gas stations, the Apache had a place for people to gamble. This was the place where she'd first put coins in a slot machine. Man. If only she could play for a few minutes. It would make her feel so much better.

"Hey, Al?"

The clerk looked up. "Yeah?"

"Mind if I drop a few quarters in the slots?" Kaylee asked.

Al nodded. "Fine with me. Just be quick."

Kaylee dug into her pockets and pulled out a five-dollar bill. "Have change?"

Al counted out some quarters as Reavis came to stand beside her. "Okay, big gambler," he said. "Let's see what you can do."

As it turned out, she couldn't do much. In less than ten

minutes, she lost all the money. But when she figured it in with last night, she was still way up. Best of all, she'd been right. A few minutes of gambling made her feel a whole lot better.

CHAPTER SIX

By the time Kaylee returned to the massive LV Skye complex, the bad feelings about Karen's arrival in Las Vegas had come roaring back. Playing the slots at the Apache Motel office had helped temporarily, but the good feeling didn't last for long.

Kaylee was full of doubts and questions. How long would her aunt stick around? Could she be prevented from coming to any part of the LV Skye, including the shopping mall? What would be the best way to do that? Did she, Kaylee, owe her aunt a job? No way would she get hired at the LV Skye. And most troubling, what was she missing? What were Karen's true intentions?

Once upon a time, she'd assumed that Karen had paid the rent with the money that Kaylee was giving her from her night job. Then she'd come home at four thirty in the morning to find they'd been evicted. That had been a big, unpleasant surprise. With Karen in Vegas, there was always a chance of another big, life-wrecking, unpleasant surprise.

She pulled up to the hotel valet, who took the Beamer from her. Then she hurried to Teen Tower. Everything seemed to be running smoothly. Everyone seemed to be having a good time.

After more than two weeks of operation, things were settling in to a regular routine. Several managers were in place to oversee the major areas of the facility. There was a dining room manager, Ellison in the gym, a game room manager, a pool deck manager, a security manager, an entertainment manager, and many others. When there weren't fires to put out, like replacing a rock drummer with the world's most upset stomach, much of what Kaylee had to do was manage the managers.

Just as she reached the pool deck, a text came in from Alana.

"Hey. Meet us at Caffeine Central. Now! Operation wedding. Want a drink?"

Us? She texted right back.

"On my way. Would love an iced almond milk latte. Thanks!"

Caffeine Central was Teen Tower's coffee garden, part

of the dining complex where Teen Tower guests could eat and drink to their hearts' content without money changing hands. It was like Starbucks on steroids, with tables, chairs, and couches inside, and round tables with umbrellas outside. Everything was cooled by misters that used the power of evaporation to chill the air. Like everything else that could be consumed at Teen Tower, Caffeine Central's drinks were high end, with coffees made from a quality of bean that a regular Starbucks could only dream about.

Since the coffee joint was so popular, it took Kaylee a few minutes to find Alana. And Zoey. And Chalice. They were at a table in the middle of all the others, shaded by a beach umbrella. Fortunately, the weather was cooler than usual for June. Though it was mid-afternoon, temps were only in the low nineties. With the evaporative cooling system in place, the dry desert air was bearable.

"Hey," Alana greeted her, and then motioned to the open fourth seat. "Got you your latte."

"Thanks," Kaylee told her. She slid into the white chair between Alana and Zoey. Zoey and Chalice greeted her. Chalice offered an actual hello, while Zoey grunted a "Hey." For Zoey Gold-Blum, this was big.

"We three are on wedding duty this afternoon," Alana told her.

"How'd the rest of the morning go?" Kaylee asked.

Zoey laughed. "Well, if you're in the catering business, the flower business, the decorating business, the video business, the publicity business, or the high-end transportation business, I would say it went well."

Wow. That was almost civil on Zoey's part, Kaylee thought.

"What Zoey's saying is that the wedding is going to be over-the-top. Abra—she's the wedding planner, you met her—has the whole thing mapped out," Alana related. "We'll do the rehearsal dinner at Mondrian, the wedding itself at the courthouse, and then the party here at the hotel. In the meantime, we have work to do. That's why you're here."

"How can I help?" Kaylee asked without hesitation. She figured that she'd either be put to work on her own or teamed up with Alana. She figured wrong.

"This afternoon, Zoey and I are meeting with the ballroom decorator. Just to make sure everything's moving along."

Kaylee nodded. "Okay. Where does that leave me?"

"With me," Chalice piped up. "We'll be together. Won't that be great? We can help each other at Teen Tower and get to know each other at the same time. It's, like, destiny!"

Kaylee groaned inwardly. The idea of spending one-on-one time with Chalice made her toenails ache. But Alana was still the boss here. "Do we have a special project?"

"Chalice will fill you in," Alana told her. "Okay, Z. We're already late. Let's go."

Without anything more, Alana and Zoey took off, taking their drinks with them. It was just Kaylee and Chalice now. Kaylee looked at the redheaded girl whose ringlets fell past her shoulders. For the first time, she realized that Chalice had green eyes. She was like a tiny, busty Barbie doll.

"So. You and me," Chalice said. "We don't really know each other. But Alana likes you. And I hear Cory likes you. So there's really no reason that I shouldn't like you too, right?"

"How do you know Cory likes me?"

Chalice smiled. "He's my friend, we talk. He says you have a lot of nice things to say about Alana."

Weird. They'd been together like two seconds, but it seemed like Chalice was opening the door to a conversation about Alana and Cory.

Kaylee took the opening. "Does he have anything to say about Alana? I mean, I'm just curious."

Chalice nodded. "He says that … well, I'm starting to

gossip now. And I shouldn't gossip. I barely know you, right?"

"I guess that's right, yeah." Kaylee was both disappointed and impressed. She felt like she'd been on the verge of really useful information for her friend and boss. That was the disappointment part. But she was impressed that Chalice decided not to go blabbing about a private conversation she presumably had with Cory. "If Cory has something to tell me about Alana, I guess he'll tell me himself."

Chalice smiled. "You live in this city long enough, you learn to keep your mouth shut. Especially when your bestie's moms run *Stripped*."

"That makes sense," Kaylee agreed. "What are we supposed to be working on today?"

"Wedding presents," Chalice said knowledgeably.

"What we're getting for Steve and Roxanne?"

She shook her head. "Nope. What the hotel shops are getting them."

Kaylee sipped her latte. The fresh almond milk was rich and delicious. "That doesn't make any sense."

Chalice laughed. "Of course it does. Our job is to go to the hotel mall and meet with the managers of all the shops. Then we find out what they're giving and make sure it's good enough. If it's not, we pick out something else."

"But that's—that's like extortion!" Kaylee blustered. "How do we possibly know if it's good enough? These people may not know Roxanne. Are they even invited to the wedding?"

"Of course they're not invited," Chalice said lightly. "Why would Steve invite them? They're shopkeepers. But that doesn't matter. They're tenants in the hotel, so giving presents like this is like a cost of doing business. What about you?"

"What about me?"

"What are you going to give?" Chalice asked.

Gulp. Kaylee swallowed hard. She hadn't actually thought about it. But she was thinking about it now. What could you buy for two rich people who already had everything?

"Dunno," Kaylee admitted.

"Think about it," Chalice told her. "Let's go."

They took the long walk to the LV Skye shopping arcade. To call it an arcade was a misnomer. It was actually like an indoor mall, full of high-end shops where people could spend their gambling winnings on clothes, jewelry, art, or tchotchkes. Many of the stores were devoted to the work of a single designer. They started in the Versace shop. The manager had read about the wedding on *Stripped* and had already picked out a his-and-hers swimsuit combination. Chalice inspected it and found it just fine.

On their way to the Diamond Mine jewelry store, Chalice asked Kaylee one more time about the wedding present.

Kaylee shook her head. "Still no clue. What about you?"

"I'm not getting them anything," Chalice declared.

"Didn't you just tell me that you have to give them something?" Kaylee felt a little sick about her own lack of ideas for a present.

They halted outside the jewelry place. "Oh, I'm giving them something. I'm just not getting them anything," Chalice explained.

"That doesn't make any sense."

"Of course it does," Chalice told Kaylee. "I'm making them something."

The idea that Chalice could make anyone anything other than credit card bills struck Kaylee as fairly absurd. "Like what?"

"Like this." Chalice opened her purse and took out her iPad. A few quick clicks later, she was on a page of thumbnail photographs. She clicked on one of them. It enlarged to an absolutely beautiful self-portrait photograph. Ah.

Chalice was going to offer Steve and Roxanne a photo session. That seemed low rent, but the photo would still be nice. Not that they needed any more pictures. But whatever. It was very thoughtful.

"You took that?"

Chalice shook her head. "Didn't take it. Painted it."

Kaylee was stunned. "You painted that? It's so real."

"Thanks. It's about five feet by three feet, by the way. Unframed. So I'm going to do one of Steve and Roxanne together," Chalice reported.

"How long will that take you?"

Chalice shrugged. "I'm pretty fast. I can work from a picture too. I'd say a few nights. I'll have it done by the wedding. Okay, let's go in."

As they went into the jewelry store, Kaylee quickly revised her opinion of Chalice Walker. Chalice was an artist. That was useful to know. She wondered why Alana had never mentioned it. And she wondered what else about this quirky little redhead she didn't know.

CHAPTER SEVEN

Two days later, the wedding of Steve Skye and Roxanne Hunter-Gibson was the talk of the town, and Kaylee found herself pressed into service more and more. The jobs she was assigned weren't glamorous. For example, she had to go to the print shop to pick up invitations.

Though the invitations were addressed—in exquisite calligraphy—there wasn't enough time for many of them to be mailed. So she and Chalice spent an incredibly boring morning logging the addresses into the messenger service's computer system. Then she and Chalice worked with the LV Skye travel office to reconfirm, one by one, the travel arrangements for those coming in from around the world for the event.

The good part of all this was that she worked with

Chalice, who was turning out to be a cheerful presence despite her many quirks. For example, Chalice was a picky eater who would not eat food on her plate that was touching and hated all fruit. For another, she had a great love of techno music. Kaylee was more into hip-hop. But she was a surprisingly hard worker who never shirked. That was important. Calling airline after airline to double-check flight times and calling rental car agencies to double-check pickup times was dull.

That's why Kaylee didn't mind when she got a phone call from her aunt asking if they could get together for a quick coffee at Dave's Diner, the breakfast and lunch place that was walking distance from the Apache Motel. To Kaylee's surprise, Karen announced that she was working there as a dishwasher.

Dave's was an old-fashioned joint that opened at five in the morning and closed at four in the afternoon. It was located in a pre-fab Airstream-style structure and had a checkerboard tile floor, red stools around a curved counter, and eight or ten booths that could seat four people each. When Kaylee pulled into the parking lot at eleven, the blacktop was half full with mostly pickup trucks and older American-made sedans. There was a sign on the door advertising both free Wi-Fi and a high Yelp rating, and the interior was sparkling clean.

Kaylee hadn't talked to Karen since she'd dropped her at the motel. She hadn't responded to Karen's plaintive text asking for a job at the LV Skye either. But Karen seemed to take no offense when she saw Kaylee enter.

"Hey, little niece!" Her aunt sat at the counter. She wore white restaurant kitchen clothes and had a hairnet on her head.

"Hi, Aunt Karen. You're working here?"

Karen laughed heartily. "Chief cook and bottle washer. Or at least dishwasher." She called to the man behind the griddle. "Hey, Dave! Come meet my little niece, Kaylee." Then she turned back to Kaylee and dropped her voice. "That's Dave, the owner. He's my boss. Be nice."

Dave—a stocky guy with two days of beard but a ready smile—came over to say hello. Karen introduced them.

"Your aunt's a gem," Dave told her.

"She is?"

"She sure is. Here early to open up. Stays late to help me shut 'er down. Never tires, never complains, and even the customers like her. She's a gem, I tell ya," Dave repeated.

"I'm ... glad to hear that." Kaylee could hardly believe that they were talking about the same Karen.

"You want a coffee?" Dave asked. Before Kaylee could answer, he was reaching for the coffee pot and pouring.

"On the house. Enjoy. Okay, big to-go order just came in. Gotta run." With a quick wave, he went back to the griddle.

"He seems nice," Kaylee ventured.

"He is," Karen gushed. "And he's single too. I mean, I'm not saying I'm interested in him. I'm just saying."

Kaylee took in her aunt. Even in the past two days, she'd changed for the better. Her eyes seemed clearer, her tremors less noticeable. She even wore a little makeup. If Kaylee didn't know her history, there was no way she could tell that her aunt had been a drug addict.

"You're looking good, Karen," she said.

"Hey. All I needed was a fresh start. Dave here gave it to me. I came in for coffee that first afternoon, and he told me his dishwasher had showed up drunk. I told him I knew how to wash dishes. And he hired me!"

Kaylee sipped her coffee, which was surprisingly rich. "Then you're lucky. I hope this works out for you." She took one more sip of coffee and thought of all the stuff back at the hotel that wasn't getting accomplished while she was away. Time was wasting. "It's great to see how well you're doing. I've got to go—"

"Don't go, please," Karen said suddenly.

"I have to go. I have work to do."

Karen swung around on her stool to face Kaylee and lowered her voice almost to a whisper. "I like Dave a lot, and I like working here. But he pays minimum wage. No one can live on that. He says after I've been here a month, he'll maybe make me a waitress, but that doesn't mean definitely."

Uh-oh. Kaylee could see where this was headed.

"Can you get me a job? At that fancy hotel? I know you can do it, Kaylee. Come on. Help me get on my feet."

Kaylee felt herself start to flush. It was mortifying to be unwilling to help her own blood. "Maybe after you've worked here for a while, Karen. Okay?"

"No. That's not okay." Karen looked over at Dave to see if he was paying attention. He wasn't, which she took as a signal to proceed. "Everyone deserves a second chance, Kaylee. When you came to Los Angeles, you had nothing. I took you in. It all kinda went south, I know, but that was then and this is now. Help me. Please. You gotta help me."

Karen took both her hands. Kaylee saw they were chapped and cracked by just a couple of days of dishwashing. Karen was working hard. That was for sure. Could Kaylee risk recommending her for work at the LV Skye? What was her obligation to this woman? And wasn't Karen right, didn't everyone deserve a second chance?

"Let me think about it," Kaylee said stiffly. She disentangled herself from Karen's hands. "I'll talk to you later."

She was glad that Karen didn't call or text her as she left the diner. She needed to get back to work, but there was a detour having to do with Karen that she wanted to make first. Instead of heading north to Las Vegas Boulevard, and then east to the LV Skye, she stopped at the Apache Motel, parked, and walked quickly to room 108, the room next to her aunt's. She knocked twice on Reavis's door, hoping he was in.

"Hey, it's Kaylee. Are you here?"

No answer. She composed a quick text for Reavis.

"Hey. It's me. Where are you?"

"Out setting up for trick tomorrow night. Will need help. U in?"

"If late, yeah. How's my aunt doing?"

Reavis texted her back. **"NP so far."**

"TY."

Kaylee pocketed her phone and headed back to the car. Truth was—she wasn't proud of this—she was looking for Reavis to give her a reason not to help her aunt. Like news that she'd been drinking, or drugging, or something. That reason wasn't there. As she pulled away from the Apache, Kaylee was more confused about Karen than ever.

That evening after Teen Tower closed, Kaylee shared the Karen story with Cory. He'd worked late in the media center, while she had beta-tested a new virtual reality game, which recreated the experience of being a gunfighter at the O.K. Corral shootout in Tombstone, Arizona. The game had been a blast, so to speak, even if Kaylee had "died" numerous times.

She and Cory ran into each other—actually, they swam into each other—in the Teen Tower pool, which was open to staff after hours. Kaylee was doing laps. Cory was diving off one of the platforms. She stopped to watch him execute a perfect swan dive, and then met him as he climbed from the pool.

Cory nodded at her predicament, even as he dripped in a pair of red surfer jams. "Tough call all around," he opined.

"What would you do?"

"I have no idea. I've never had a relative who was a meth head."

"You should have seen her back in Los Angeles," Kaylee told him. "She was a nightmare."

"The question is, how big a risk do you want to take? If she's really clean, I think Alana probably would give her a job if you insisted. She could be a dishwasher here. But if she blew it, it's on you."

Kaylee flipped her head to one side to free some water that had settled in her left ear. "I don't really want to take any risk."

"Then I think you know what to do."

Kaylee nodded. The answer was clear. She just had to be willing to take on Karen's dismay, even if it meant being hard-nosed. "She can't work here. Not for a long time. A year. And that's only if she stays clean. She needs to prove she's got her life on track for a year, not just for two days."

"I think you're making the right decision. Now let's swim."

Cory pointed to the pool. They jumped in and treaded water side by side. Kaylee realized she had another chance now to explore where Cory stood with Alana. Maybe he and Alana had been hanging out together. Or maybe he'd at least been thinking about Alana. She realized that she'd love to have something good to report about Cory to Alana, who was all stressed out over the wedding.

"Have you seen Alana at all? It's like she's working two jobs these days. What with the wedding and all."

Cory shook his head. "Not much. Here at Teen Tower, that's it."

"Hey. Maybe she could use your help with the wedding stuff," Kaylee suggested. "She's such an awesome girl."

"She hasn't asked me."

Kaylee smiled knowingly. "She's not going to ask.

Girls don't ask. She's waiting for you to offer."

Cory swam over to the edge of the pool and held onto the concrete rim. Kaylee followed.

"Did that upset you?" Kaylee asked him.

Cory shook his head. "Nah. I already know about girls and guys. Probably more than you do."

For the second time that day, Kaylee felt her face start to flush. "I think that's a little harsh."

"Not really." He smiled. "If you knew more about guys and girls, you would probably realize what I'm about to tell you. At this point in my life, I think I'm more interested in you than I am in Alana. In fact, I don't think I am. I know I am."

Kaylee gulped. She didn't know what to say to that, so she said nothing. She liked Cory too. She knew that she could really *like* him. Her allegiance, though, was to Alana. No way could she pursue anything with Cory unless Alana said it would be okay. And no way, she realized, would that *ever* happen.

CHAPTER EIGHT

From that time on, Kaylee didn't want any drama, so she did her best not to be seen in Cory's presence by anyone around the hotel. She minimized her own contact with him. That part of her work life went reasonably well. The part that didn't go so well was having Zoey around Teen Tower and around Alana.

As the wedding prep got more intense, Kaylee saw how close Alana was getting with her old friend. It happened in subtle ways. Alana used to come to talk to Kaylee alone. These days, Zoey was always in tow. When Alana had lunch with the teen kids of a foreign leader who'd been invited to the wedding, Zoey had been invited to join her, not Kaylee.

Hardest of all for Kaylee was how Alana talked all the

time about Zoey's great ideas for Teen Tower. Coming up with great ideas had been Kaylee's job, so she redoubled her efforts. She even created a plan for what they should do if and when Reavis got a regular magician's gig at Teen Tower. It was her idea to have him perform at the very end of the day to try to keep kids on the premises for the maximum amount of time and their parents in the hotel casino. All Alana commented was that it was a nice idea about something that might never happen.

Kaylee tried not to let all this get her down for more than five minutes. She had a job to do. But one way or another, what was unspoken would have to be spoken. About Zoey. About her and Cory. About everything.

It actually felt good to leave Teen Tower the next night and meet up with Reavis a.k.a. Phantom. He'd been wowing the town in a series of hit-and-run public magic acts for weeks, with Kaylee as his assistant.

She'd helped him perform outside Penn and Teller's show at the Rio Hotel, crash the pirate act in the lagoon outside the Treasure Island Hotel and Casino, and even do the unannounced performance that had wowed the Teen Tower opening day crowd. In less than a month, Reavis had made a great rep for himself in his secret Phantom identity. Kaylee knew of just four people who were now aware that Phantom was Reavis: herself, Alana, Jamila, and Greg. Everyone had kept their mouths shut so far. But who knew how long that would last?

Kaylee really wanted Reavis to let her try to get him a gig at the LV Skye. He held out. He wanted to do more hit-and-run shows and build even more publicity. He claimed that the moment public opinion was at a fever pitch would be his moment to strike.

Kaylee believed that there was another reason he was hesitating. She brought it up as they drove in his Toyota RAV4 to the destination of that night's performance, Cashman Field, where the Las Vegas 51s played baseball. The 51s were the Las Vegas Triple-A minor league team. They always attracted a big crowd of tourists and locals to their night games. Day games in the summer were out of the question. The stadium would just be too hot under the blazing desert sun.

"You're still not ready for me to talk to Alana and Steve about you?" she asked.

Reavis shook his head. He was dressed in dark clothes and a long duster coat. Before he got out of the car, he would don the Phantom mask that hid his face. The mask actually made performing harder because he couldn't use his face to misdirect the audience away from what he didn't want them to see. "Nope. Time isn't right."

"I think the time is exactly right," Kaylee said pointedly.

"We don't have a magician on the entertainment staff at Teen Tower. Not yet. But you know it's going to happen. Why shouldn't it be you?"

"Because if I go in to Steve Skye now," Reavis said, "he'll laugh at me. I auditioned for him a couple of years ago. I bombed. That's why I'm wearing the mask." He frowned. "One thing about magic. There are no second chances. You screw up the trick, it's wrecked. It's a horrible feeling. Same thing with an audition."

"When will you know it's the right time?"

"I'll know."

The baseball field was northeast of downtown. It took quite a while to drive there. Reavis had been out to the parking lot the previous day and had set up the props for the trick. They drove without speaking the rest of the way with the 51s's game on the radio. They were playing a team from Salt Lake City. Kaylee and Reavis timed their arrival perfectly—the 51s were batting in the bottom of the ninth inning. They didn't even have to pay for parking since the attendants had long since left the collection booths at the parking lot entrance.

Reavis went over the trick with Kaylee one more time before they got out of the car. "Optical illusion tonight with the help of a high-tech blanket I had made in Taiwan. This crowd's gonna eat it up. Criss Angel has a trick where he pulls people in two. I'm going to pull you into *three*. Thank you for wearing all blue. It helps with the illusion."

Kaylee had worn blue jeans and a blue long-sleeve T-shirt, as Reavis had asked. "How does this blanket thing work?"

Reavis laughed. "You're asking me to give away my secrets? Are you kidding? Your eyes are going to be closed. Close them when I ask you to do that. Keep 'em that way. But you're going to feel a handle on the bottom of the blanket I'm going to cover you with. When I press on your tummy, count silently to three, and then yank down on the handle. It'll activate the optics in the blanket."

"Pull the handle. Got it," Kaylee told him.

"Yep. When I start my patter, you blend into the crowd. I'll pick you out like you're just any volunteer—you'll be the second person I ask—we do the trick and go home. Have some fun with me when I talk to you. Good?"

Kaylee got the familiar shiver of excitement in her stomach. It happened every time that she helped Reavis perform. "Totally good."

"Hopefully a lot of people will video it on their cell phones," Reavis said. "I want twenty videos posted on YouTube."

"And on the *Stripped* blog," Kaylee added helpfully.

"Especially on *Stripped*," Reavis agreed.

Ten minutes later the ballgame was over. The 51s had won on a walk-off home run in the bottom of the ninth inning, so the people streaming out of the stadium were in a happy mood. Kaylee stood off to one side as Reavis worked to attract an audience. He'd donned his mask and was calling to the crowd as they headed for their cars.

"Hello, Las Vegas! It's your lucky night! You get to see Phantom perform! Hurry, hurry! Text it and tweet it! Show starts in two minutes! Hurry, hurry, hurry!"

That was all the prompting Reavis needed to draw an immense crowd. Quite a few people at the stadium had heard of Phantom. The ones who hadn't were filled in by their excited friends. Within a couple of minutes, a massive semicircle of baseball fans had formed around Reavis, who had parked his vehicle near a pre-positioned bench at the farthest reaches of the parking lot where they wouldn't be bothered by exiting cars.

As planned, Kaylee wandered into the center of the crowd, trying to look like just any other spectator. Meanwhile, Reavis was keeping the crowd in stitches with patter about the erotic life of Harry Houdini and how great it must have been to be his wife, Bess. "But enough about that. It's time for my trick. Who's gonna help me?"

A hundred hands went in the air. To Kaylee and the crowd's delight, Reavis approached a pre-teen girl and got her parents' permission to bring her forward. The crowd cheered. Then he positioned the girl on the bench, stepped back, and shook his head sadly. "Sorry, sweetheart. You're too short for this trick. You need to grow. Go to Alex Rodriguez and borrow some human growth hormone. Ooh! I did not just say that. I am the worst person in the world!"

The crowd roared with laughter as Reavis bowed, brought the girl back to her parents, and then asked for another volunteer. More hands, including Kaylee's, were raised. This time, Reavis picked Kaylee out of the crowd. Nobody blinked. No one suspected that Kaylee was a plant. He'd done a verbal and emotional misdirect with the little kid. So far, so good.

"Hey, sweetheart," he said to Kaylee like he didn't know her. "You really want to help me? It's taking your life in your hands."

"I think I can handle you, Phantom," Kaylee said sassily.

The crowd laughed.

"I'd like for you to handle me," Reavis shot back, resulting in more mirth.

"Where's the embalming fluid?"

The audience roared with laughter at Kaylee's joke.

"We'll see what kind of shape you're in to embalm anyone when this trick is over," Reavis said, and then motioned for Kaylee to stretch out on the bench. She did, then closed her eyes on Reavis's command. He kept talking as he spread a blanket over her. Just as he'd promised, she felt a plastic handle on the bottom of the blanket.

"And now, ladies, gentlemen, and baseball fans, I need absolute silence. I give you, the Great Expanding Girl! Close your eyes, young lady. No embalming."

Kaylee closed her eyes. She heard the tap-tap of footsteps as Reavis approached her, followed by the pressure of his hands on her tummy. She counted to three and then pulled the handle on the bottom of the blanket.

The crowd screamed like they'd just seen someone torn into three before their eyes. Because—Reavis told her this later—that's what they'd seen, for a split-second anyway. There were special pressure-sensitive optical fibers in the blanket that were activated when Kaylee pulled the handle. The crowd didn't know that. She heard the reaction, though. And then the thunderous applause when it seemed to the audience like her body had reattached perfectly.

"Thank you, thank you!" Reavis said as he helped Kaylee to her feet. "I'm Phantom, and thank you very much! Take a bow, young lady!"

Kaylee bowed. Reavis bowed again, and the cheering

got louder. Kaylee saw that many people had their cell phones out, taking video of the performance so they could show their friends or post it online. Well, that was cool. That was part of the fun of performing in public, and it was just what Reavis wanted.

Then came trouble.

When they talked about it later, Reavis and Kaylee realized they should have been smart enough to be prepared for what happened. But they weren't prepared when a young guy in his twenties, who'd had three or four beers too many at the baseball game, burst out of the crowd and came straight at Reavis and Kaylee. Reavis stepped in front of Kaylee to protect her, but the guy's target wasn't Kaylee. It was Reavis himself.

"Show your face, dork!" he screamed at Reavis and tore at his mask.

"Get away from me, you jerk!" Reavis bellowed and tried to hustle Kaylee away to safety.

The guy kept pace, though, then turned to the crowd and yelled. "Come on, help me out here! Don'tcha wanna see who he is? Let's get his mask off!"

As Kaylee watched in horror, several other young men charged out of the crowd to join the drunk guy. Reavis got into a shoving match with some of them and barely kept the mask on his face. Kaylee stepped into the fray. She felt rough hands grab at her too. Disaster seemed imminent until the wail of sirens interrupted the action. With lights flashing, a ballpark security vehicle approached. One of the drunk guys called to his friends, "Run, dudes!"

They ran. So did Reavis and Kaylee. Straight back to the car. She got to the driver's side of the vehicle, climbed in, and started the engine as Reavis grabbed his magic blanket and jumped into the passenger seat.

"Go, go, go," Reavis demanded.

She peeled out of the parking space and gunned the car toward the entrance to the parking lot.

"Jeezly," Reavis exclaimed. "What a mess. You could've been hurt!"

"That's why I've been telling you to get a regular gig."

Kaylee steamed as she drove out of the parking lot and back toward the hotel where Reavis would drop her before he continued to the Apache Motel. What was it about men? Why were they such stubborn idiots? Why did they make such bad decisions?

"I want to help you," she told him as they pulled up in front of the LV Skye. "But I can't help you if you don't take my help."

"I get it," Reavis told her.

Kaylee shook her head. "No, you don't. I don't think you understand at all."

"Kaylee?"

"Yeah?" Her voice was wary.

"If you're still up for it?" he asked. "Set up that meeting about me working at Teen Tower. I'm ready."

CHAPTER NINE

The first thing Kaylee did the morning after the baseball stadium fiasco was check *Stripped*. She'd seen all those people taking video the night before, and she fully expected that there would be links to what happened on the blog. Zoey's mothers did not disappoint. There wasn't just one video there, there were several. The headline read, "Ballpark Melee for Phantom."

Then she texted Reavis. When he'd dropped her off, he claimed he was ready for her to make an effort to get him a gig at Teen Tower. She wondered if he was feeling the same way by the dawn's early light.

"U awake?"

"Yeah."

"U still up to do what you gotta do?"

"Yeah."

That was the answer she was looking for.

"Then I'm setting it up."

"Yeah."

"I'll tell you what time."

"Yeah."

She clicked off and texted Cory. She needed all the support she could get. It was time Cory knew about Reavis's secret identity. Then she composed an e-mail to Alana. It was one that she'd been hoping to send for a long time. The events of the night before now made it possible. She understood Reavis's reluctance. He'd humiliated himself in front of Steve Skye once, and now he was back for more. Kaylee hadn't been there to see Reavis's original audition, but she knew that Steve did not suffer fools lightly. Or, she suspected, magicians who didn't meet his high standards.

> To: Alana
>
> From: Kaylee
>
> Re: Phantom
>
> Hey and good morning. Hope all is good. Did you read about Reavis's show last night at the ballpark? Disaster, almost. We got away, but he was nearly unmasked and beaten up too. It's in *Stripped*. So listen, I think I've finally convinced

him that he needs to talk to your father about a regular gig. I want him at Teen Tower every day as a closing act, and I think you do too. No way this happens without your dad. I'm sure your dad is full-frontal busy with the wedding, but I think we should do the meeting f-a-s-t before Reavis changes his mind. Can you set it up?

-K

The response came five minutes later by text. Alana had pulled it together, and pulled it together quickly.

"Good. See U 10 am SS office. He should be ready 2 do tricks."

She texted back to Alana. **"Does SS know Reavis is Phantom?"**

"No," Alana answered. **"And he won't till the audition is over."**

That was what Kaylee had been looking for. She let Reavis know that she'd meet him in the hotel lobby at nine thirty. They could walk together to Steve's office. He should come in street clothes and bring a performance outfit and his mask. He needed to be prepared to do some tricks if Steve wanted.

Kaylee got to the hotel lobby five minutes early. Reavis was right on time, wearing dark slacks and a black button-down shirt and carrying a green duffel bag. Kaylee thought he looked glum.

"Why the long face?" she asked. "You're going to kill this."

"I'm not feeling it today," Reavis muttered.

Okay. That was a bad start. She hadn't done all this work, put all her faith in him, for him not to feel it. "You don't have to feel it," she told him, trying to be supportive. "You just have to do it."

He didn't say anything to that, so she stopped walking. Reavis kept going for a few steps until he realized Kaylee wasn't keeping pace.

"What?" he asked her after he'd turned around.

She put her hands on her hips and looked him in the eye. "You know what? Everybody in life needs a break unless their name is Alana Skye. I got my break from Alana, but then it was up to me to make the most of it. I haven't always done great, but I've always given it everything I've got. This is your break. I haven't even told Alana that you auditioned for her dad before because I didn't want anything in the way of this happening. Let him find out it's you after you audition. You gotta give it everything you've got."

He smiled wanly. "What if I break the big break? I've done it before, it could happen again."

"Please. What happened with Steve Skye last time was practice. This is real. I can't guarantee how it's going to turn out. No one can. But I need to know that you're going to give it everything you've got." She relaxed. "Okay. That's the end of my speech."

He grinned at her with appreciation. "You're not just a girl, Kaylee. You're a concept."

"I'm just doing you a favor. You with me?"

Reavis nodded. "I'm with you. Who's going to be at this meeting?"

"Me. Alana. Cory, I think—I hope you don't mind that I told him. You."

"Nah, it's okay. It's just … the big boss …"

"He intimidates everyone, Reavis. Yes, the big boss will be there too."

Reavis seemed to steel himself. "Okay. Let's do this."

Together, they strode purposefully through the rest of the lobby, down to the hotel business wing, and into Steve Skye's suite of offices. Just before they went inside, Reavis put on his Phantom performance mask. As usual, Steve's executive assistant, Mrs. Rogers, was at her desk. She was guardian of Steve's kingdom. As Kaylee had expected, Cory and Alana were in Steve's reception area. The surprise was who else had shown up. More than a surprise. Totally upending. Shocking, actually.

Zoey Gold-Blum.

Before she said a word to anyone, Kaylee followed the logic in her head. Zoey was there. Therefore, Zoey was coming to the meeting. Therefore, Zoey knew what the meeting was about. Therefore, someone had talked to Zoey about the subject of the meeting. Therefore, Alana had talked to Zoey and told her that Phantom was Reavis. All this had been done without Alana ever discussing it with Kaylee. What was up with that?

"Who's the other girl?" Reavis muttered.

"Zoey, she's a friend of Alana's." Kaylee stared razor-sharp daggers at Alana. "Can we talk?" Kaylee asked her boss.

"We are talking," Alana told her.

Kaylee struggled to keep her anger under control. She had to manage both Reavis and the situation. Reavis was already nervous. She didn't want to do anything to make that even worse. "I mean privately."

She saw Alana glance at Mrs. Rogers, who pointed to the clock. "If you're all here, your dad can call you in at any time. Don't go far."

Great. It was earlier than the time Steve had called the meeting for. But with all the parties there, there was no good reason to delay any longer. Whatever she had to say to Alana, she had to say it fast.

"Fine," Alana said. "Come outside."

Kaylee was the first one out of the room. Alana followed her into the corridor. Kaylee made sure that the soundproof door was closed before she turned to her boss. "What is *she* doing here?"

"Zoey?"

"No," Kaylee said, unable to contain her sarcasm. She realized that Alana was her boss, but she was so angry. "Justin Bieber in drag. Of course, Zoey!"

Alana looked at her with steely eyes. "I'm in charge of Teen Tower. I thought it would help to have her here with us. To convince my dad, that is. We'll find out soon if I'm right."

Kaylee fumed. Yes, Alana was the boss. That was true. But this whole thing had been engineered by Kaylee, which meant she had a right to fair warning. She should have known that Alana was planning to bring Zoey. What good would it do for Zoey to be at this meeting, if Reavis was so freaked out that he was unable to audition? Nothing should be left to chance, and Alana had opted to take a big chance. Plus, there was the whole issue of Reavis's secret identity. It was even more compromised now.

"Zoey knows who Phantom is—that it's Reavis. She could go to her moms, and then they'll put it in the blog, and then the whole secret identity thing will get wrecked."

Alana set her jaw in a way that made Kaylee realize she'd made no headway with her boss. Not that she knew exactly what she wanted, given the situation. Steve would be ready for them in a minute or two. It was impossible to send Zoey away now. Like at the roulette table, the little ball had gone into the wheel. Where it would land would be anyone's guess.

"Look," Alana finally said. "You may be good at the hospitality business, but you don't know my father like I do. If you want Reavis to get hired, you want Zoey in this meeting. If you don't, then you don't. It's as simple as that."

"She better not wreck it," Kaylee warned.

The door to the corridor opened. Mrs. Rogers stuck her head outside. "Your dad's ready for you," she told Alana.

"Okay," Alana said. "We're coming."

They all filed into Steve's conference room. But he wasn't there yet.

They sat in nervous silence. Reavis and Zoey on one side of Alana. Kaylee and Cory on the other. Kaylee scanned the conference room, with its long mahogany table, leather chairs, and video monitors, both for recording and playback. There were crystal glasses and pitchers of ice water on the table. Though her throat had suddenly gone dry, she didn't dare pour herself a glassful for fear that she'd spill it.

They had to wait a couple of minutes for Steve. When he entered, Kaylee saw him register mild surprise at the size of the entourage. Then she looked at Reavis. Steve took him in with amusement. It was a good thing that he wasn't a more careful observer, Kaylee decided. If he'd bothered to take in Reavis's hands, he would have seen that Phantom was trembling from nervousness.

Steve Skye sat across the table. He was dressed in a custom made dark suit, white shirt, and yellow tie. He looked like money because he was money.

Steve addressed Alana. "You called this meeting. You start it." He took off his Rolex and put it on the table in front of him. "But I'm a busy man, and I'm getting married this weekend. You've got fifteen minutes."

Kaylee looked down the table at Alana, wondering how she was going to start the presentation. To her shock, Alana turned to Zoey.

"Zoey, you know Vegas," Alana said nonchalantly. "Why don't you tell my dad why we're here?"

No, Kaylee thought. No, no, no.

This was *totally* the wrong way to begin.

CHAPTER TEN

At the prompt from Alana, Kaylee saw Zoey grin like she was a school girl who'd just nabbed Justin Timberlake as her prom date. Because Reavis wore his Phantom mask, she couldn't gauge his reaction to this unexpected development. Then she noticed his hands. They had balled into fists. He was mad that Kaylee hadn't been asked to speak first. Very mad.

"Thanks, Alana," Zoey said, addressing Alana instead of Steve. "And let me say first what an honor it has been to work for you during these last few days. Because of your dad's wedding, you've been busier than any girl should be. I'm thrilled to have been able to step in and take up some of the slack."

"You're welcome," Alana said. Kaylee's anger sizzled

even more. Zoey was talking like she was now Alana's prime Teen Tower aide instead of Kaylee. Well, maybe that was what was going on here. This was Zoey's debut party, and Kaylee hadn't realized she was invited to the festivities until it had already started.

"Cut to the chase and end the love fest, girls," Steve told them. "You didn't come here to put makeup on each other."

"No, we didn't," Zoey told him as Kaylee sat by helplessly. "We're here because we have a chance to hire the hottest magician in town to come and work at Teen Tower. You've read about Phantom in my moms' blog. He's this guerilla magician. Hit and run. At Penn and Teller's show. Then at the Palms, where I filmed him. Then he walked on water at Treasure Island. The Teen Tower opening, of course. Other spectacular tricks around town before he did this thing at the ballpark ... for which, I must say, his assistant looked a lot like Kaylee Ryan. I'm just saying."

Steve nodded. "I've seen the video. Your moms posted it. If I have an issue with Alana's assistant, I'll take it up with Alana and her assistant, thank you very much."

"Fair enough," Zoey acknowledged. "Excuse me." With extreme confidence, she reached forward, poured herself a goblet of ice water, and brought the goblet to her lips without spilling a drop. "Thank you. So, to continue,

Phantom is the magician the whole city is talking about. Phantom is doing tricks that no one else can do. Phantom has the goods and the attitude. He has mystery. He'll bring even more people to Teen Tower. Alana and I are proposing that he work every evening right before closing in a half-hour show at the Teen Tower main stage"

Kaylee's super-heated blood reached the boiling point. It had been *Kaylee's* concept that Reavis would perform at the end of the Teen Tower day. Alana and Zoey appropriated it!

Steve sat back in the leather chair that dwarfed all the others and folded his arms. Kaylee saw him fix his eyes on Cory.

"Cory, what do you think?" he asked.

"I'm in favor, sir," Cory responded.

"You agree with everything?" Steve pressed.

"With everything. I have to say, I've never heard as much buzz about a magician since David Blaine got started," Cory told him. "I think if you hire Phantom, this could be the start of a franchise."

Kaylee loved Cory's answer. Short, direct, and to the point. Then, Steve shifted his attention to her.

"What about you, Kaylee? Or does your special relationship with Phantom mean you can't be objective?"

Kaylee was about to answer when Reavis broke in.

"She doesn't have a special relationship with me. She helps me with my tricks. That's all."

Steve smiled. "When I'm ready to talk to you, I'll talk to you, Reavis. Now, Kaylee? I asked you a question."

There was a collective, audible gasp in the room. Yes, Steve had asked Kaylee a question. But answering it was impossible as everyone in the room, including Kaylee, was shocked. Steve had addressed Reavis by his real name, which meant that Steve knew Phantom's identity. How he knew it, and how he'd found it out, was a mystery. But he knew it. Which meant that Steve knew Reavis had already auditioned for him and blown that audition.

Even before Kaylee could answer, Reavis sheepishly took off his mask. His face looked bloodless. Steve grinned.

"We meet again," Steve said to him.

"Yes we do," Reavis responded.

"You're a better magician now, I understand."

"Yes, sir. I believe I am," Reavis agreed.

"How did you find out his real name?" Kaylee asked Steve.

Steve laughed. "Oh, please. I've known it since he did that mystery show at the Teen Tower opening with you."

"But how?"

Steve tapped on an iPad in front of him. The lights

in the conference room dimmed by half. Then he tapped again and a rear-view, close-up photograph of Reavis's sport SUV came up on one of the video screens. The license plate from Texas was clearly visible.

"This is a digression, Kaylee, but since you asked, we take photos of every vehicle coming in and out of our parking lot. After opening day, we looked at all the cars coming and going from Teen Tower. Once we identified Reavis's car, it was no problem to trace the plate." He grinned at Reavis. "You have to do better on your misdirection." Then he shifted back to Kaylee. "You agree that I should make Reavis a headliner?"

Kaylee nodded. "Yes, sir. With all my heart. And I won't have to risk my life helping him with his tricks ever again."

Steve laughed. When it was clear that his laughter was sincere, everyone else laughed too. Even Zoey. Even Reavis.

"I promise, Kaylee, that I'll have a different assistant," Reavis quipped. Kaylee could tell he was feeling more confident, like he had weathered the storm. Alas, Steve wasn't done with him.

"Not so fast." Steve held up his hand. "Everyone, you need to watch this."

He touched the iPad again. The lights dimmed again.

Almost instantly, a video started to play on the largest of the display screens. The scene was in this same conference room. The camera was focused on a two-years-younger Reavis, who was doing tricks for some unviewed people. That it was more than one person was obvious from the background talk and the laughter. The laughter was not at Reavis's magician patter or at the brilliance of Reavis's tricks. No. The laughter was mean and scornful because Reavis failed at trick after trick.

Cards spewed all over the table. Disappearing balls didn't disappear but rolled out of Reavis's hands and onto the floor. When Reavis tried to make a baby chicken appear from his magician's top hat, the chick refused to come out, and then it pooped in Reavis's hand when it did. Reavis got more and more embarrassed as the "show" went on. Finally, after apologizing to everyone in the room, he packed up his things and slinked away.

Kaylee chanced a sidelong glance at Reavis, who was intently watching this horror show in which he was the unwilling star. His face was stony, his eyes unblinking. Inside, though, Kaylee knew he had to be suffering terribly.

When the tape was over, Steve brought the lights back up to full. "That's the great Reavis, in this very room two years ago."

"I'm better than that, sir," Reavis said.

Steve nodded. "That might be true. I saw you at the Teen Tower opening up on that balcony. You did that illusion of decapitating Kaylee. Damned impressive. I've also seen clips from the last few weeks."

"Thank you, sir."

"You're welcome." Steve leaned forward and put both hands on the table in front of him. "But the fact remains, you cracked when you auditioned for me. Cracked badly, in fact. Which scares me. And I don't like to be scared."

"He's a different magician now," Kaylee interjected. She wanted to do something to support Reavis.

Steve shook his head. "No. He's the same magician with more experience. But his heart is the same. Do you know how embarrassing it will be for me to have him crack like that on the main stage? Do you know who they'll blame?"

"Me," Alana jumped into the debate. "I asked for this meeting."

"No! Me!" Steve thundered. Then he seemed to make a decision. He pointed to the far end of the conference room and then to Reavis. "You brought some of your act with you?"

Reavis nodded.

"Then give us a trick. And put your mask back on. I like that Phantom thing. Go."

Everyone watched, rapt, as Reavis slipped on his mask and moved to the front of the room. He took some balls out of his pocket and started juggling them. Then, disaster struck. One of the balls dropped onto the table and rolled away.

"I'm sorry," Reavis said sheepishly.

Kaylee felt sick to her stomach. Reavis was cracking under the pressure again. What was going on with him? Did he have stage fright? And if he did, why didn't he have it in front of hundreds, or even thousands, of people?

"Go on," Steve instructed. "More."

Reavis put away the balls. Kaylee literally held her breath.

"I'm going to do the same card trick as two years ago," Reavis declared. He took a deck of cards out of his pocket and started to shuffle. The shuffling was dazzling in and of itself, and Kaylee started to relax. He could do this. He was going to do this. Steve was going to offer him a Teen Tower gig. Everything was going to be better than fine.

As he was shuffling for what looked like the last time, the magic gremlins—or Reavis's nerves—struck again. The cards spewed out from his hands like grass from a lawnmower without a catch-bag. They flew to the table, to the floor, to the chairs. Almost like it was fate, a card landed facedown directly in front of Steve.

Kaylee felt terrible. What a mess. What an embarrassment. What a blown opportunity. She felt like she was personally responsible for it too. This couldn't help her reputation with Steve or Alana.

Steve spoke up. "Reavis, you can spare yourself a lot of embarrassment if you'd just leave now. And don't come back. You obviously haven't gotten your nerves together in two years of prep. Maybe you can work birthday parties."

Reavis, though, was smiling oddly. He seemed unfazed. Calm. Centered, like any magician should be.

"There's a card in front of you, Mr. Skye."

Steve looked at the facedown card. "I can see that."

"If I didn't know better, I'd say it was the ace of hearts. But it's facedown, so I couldn't know better. But maybe you know better. Can you turn it over please?"

As Steve went to flip the card over, Kaylee exulted. This was some kind of a trick, and Reavis had planned the whole thing. It was supposed to appear like he'd flubbed again, but instead, he had executed the greatest card trick of all time. Genius. So much genius.

The room buzzed as Steve smiled, then turned the card over and displayed it. It was an ace.

Unfortunately, it was the ace of spades.

Everyone moaned a little. Even Steve seemed disappointed. Reavis, though, didn't flinch.

"Wrong card," Reavis said. "I meant the one in your lap."

Steve looked down. Evidently, there was a card in his lap because he lifted it up and turned it over. His jaw opened in surprise. Ace of hearts.

"How'd you do that," Steve demanded. "How?"

"Skills, sir," Reavis replied.

"That is an impossible trick."

Reavis grinned. "And yet I made it happen."

Steve stood. "Meeting's over. I'll let you know."

He left. When he was gone, Kaylee departed with Reavis and Cory. Kaylee and Cory each complimented Reavis on his great trick. Kaylee didn't say anything about what had come before it, though, when Reavis had messed up the trick with the balls. The flying cards had been brilliant. The balls had been a mess. Would Steve Skye overlook the mistake and focus on the brilliance? Or would he focus on the mistake and overlook the brilliance? She didn't know, and she had no way of finding out. When Steve said he'd be in touch, it was his way of saying that the choice was his, and he'd make it on his own timetable.

The two of them walked Reavis to the valet stand. When Reavis's car pulled up, he thanked them again and drove off, leaving Cory and Kaylee alone.

"That was a surprise," Cory told her.

"That he was so good, or that he was so bad?"

"Neither. It was a surprise that Zoey was there."

"I think maybe I'm obsolete," Kaylee said.

He touched her arm. "You're definitely obsolete if we don't get to Teen Tower and get to work. Come on."

It was weird in the best possible way. Kaylee did feel as if she was less important these days than Zoey. It scared and upset her. Zoey didn't like her one bit. Zoey probably didn't like that she was hanging out with Chalice either. If Zoey really got in Alana's ear, she might suggest that Teen Tower could function just fine without Kaylee. And then Kaylee might find herself without a job.

That would be terrible, she realized, but it wouldn't put her in an impossible situation. She was a different girl from the one who had arrived in Vegas a few weeks before. She was smarter and more confident. She had come to town with nothing, but now she had resources. She had friends like Jamila and Greg and Cory and Chalice. If she got canned or replaced, they would help her. It would hurt, yeah. But she'd be okay.

Still, she hoped she'd never have to find out.

CHAPTER ELEVEN

Kaylee woke the next morning far earlier than usual. There was no good reason for her to be up at six. The night before, she and Chalice had gone to see a new Judd Apatow comedy. Chalice proved to be surprisingly good company. After the movie, she'd taken Kaylee to her favorite Thai restaurant where they'd snacked on *som tam* salads and drank Thai iced tea. Kaylee was back to her room by ten thirty and asleep at her regular bedtime.

Normally, she had a room service breakfast, but that wasn't due to be delivered for another seventy-five minutes. Instead, she made coffee with the coffeemaker in the wet bar, checked the *Stripped* blog, and answered a few e-mails. By that time it was six thirty. There were still forty-five minutes until breakfast arrived. With so much time, she decided that she'd make the most of it. She could go to the Teen Tower gym for a workout and maybe even spend a short time in the sauna or steam room. She changed into gym clothes and called the kitchen, asking them to hold breakfast until 7:45 a.m. Then she took the elevator down to the hotel lobby, walked through the lobby and the casino, heading for the gym.

As she passed the casino, though, her usual fascination kicked in. It was the least likely time for anyone to gamble—before breakfast, and certainly before most people vacationing in Vegas would even be awake—but there were still plenty of people at the slot machines and the gaming tables. Security was lax, probably because there weren't many people coming and going at this hour. Kaylee had no trouble finding an entrance to the casino floor where no guards were stopping people below the minimum age or who were visibly inebriated. She just walked in like she belonged there.

As usual, the place was thrilling in a way she barely understood. It was sensory overload. Bright lights, loud rock music, the sounds of slot machines paying off winners. It smelled of perfume, perspiration, alcohol, cigarettes, and money.

With her head buzzing slightly from an adrenaline rush, she wandered around with no goal in mind. The before-breakfast crowd was an odd cross-section of humanity: chubby women in shorts and T-shirts, well-dressed Japanese tourists, young guys in sunglasses even though they were indoors, and middle-aged men wearing chinos and desperate looks.

There was no chance of Kaylee gambling. She hadn't even brought a quarter with her, just her room keycard. She did stop, though, to watch a middle-aged Asian woman play intently at a slot machine based on the TV game show "Wheel of Fortune." Finally, the woman noticed her.

"Hey there, honey," she said to Kaylee with a Southern accent that Kaylee didn't expect. "You havin' a good ol' night?"

Kaylee nodded. "So far, so good. Can I ask you something?"

The woman nodded. "Sure, go ahead, but that don't automatically mean I'm gonna answer you!"

"You said 'night.' How long have you been playing?"

"What time is it?" the woman asked.

"About six forty-five in the morning."

The woman looked a little surprised. "It's that late? Or early? Or something? I guess I lost track of the time. Goodness me!" She grinned wickedly. "Just havin' too much fun for one human bein', I guess."

"Is it okay if I ask if you're up or down?"

"Down on the night, up on the trip," the woman reported proudly. She pushed the button to spin the "Wheel of Fortune" wheels on the machine. It came up a loser, and she pushed again. Small win this time.

"When did you come to Vegas? How long has this trip been?" Kaylee asked.

"Got here five days ago." The woman pushed the button again. Kaylee watched. It was another loser.

"How many hours a day do you play?"

The woman laughed. "About ten hours a day, I reckon."

"That's a lot of time to be in here," Kaylee observed. "What else do you do while you're in Vegas?"

"Eat at the buffet, see a show or two. But really? This is the only place I want to be. Right here. In this lucky seat, doing this. Not a care in the world except the wheels going round and round. Feel bad if I lose, feel good if I win. Simple, right?"

Kaylee nodded. She craved that feeling of simplicity. She hadn't had anything close to a simple life. Raised by her grandmother, her mom was dead, her father in prison, her aunt a meth head. She'd never even lived in the same dwelling for more than two years at a time. It was so stressful. Even now, when it looked like life had come up blackjack for her and she had this great job here at the hotel, it wasn't simple.

She could have hung out more and watched the woman gamble, but she got nervous that casino security would throw her out and report her to Steve Skye. So she said good-bye and made her way over to Teen Tower. The guards there let her in with waves and smiles, and she crossed the pool deck toward the gym.

She expected it to be empty, but that's not what she found. In fact, as she stepped inside, she was stunned by what she saw. Actually, not what she saw. *Who* she saw.

About halfway back toward the weight machines was Alana. She wore gym shorts and a sports-bra top. With her was Ellison in workout gear of his own. Ellison was training Alana.

As Kaylee watched, it became clear that this was no ordinary training, but one that included plenty of hands-on attention by the trainer toward the trainee—who seemed to be enjoying it. Ellison was having Alana do squats with a barbell with light weights attached. She held it across her neck. He assisted her down and back up, and his hands weren't just on Alana's waist.

Kaylee moved to one side of the gym so she could observe out of sight. Ellison moved Alana to a leg-press machine. All the time, one of his hands was on her. Touching her back, touching her arm, touching her shoulder. Kaylee could hear his constant encouragement, telling Alana how fine she was, that she was getting stronger every day, how she was going to be the hottest girl at Teen Tower if he had anything to do with it.

Her mind reeled. Alana was getting stronger every day? What did that mean? It had to mean that Ellison had been training Alana for a while. When had this started? Did Cory know? Did it even matter if Cory knew?

Then she watched Ellison kiss Alana. She kissed him back with distinct enthusiasm.

Whoa, baby.

Kaylee wanted to get out of there and think. But her subconscious mind had other plans. That was the only reasonable explanation for why she smashed a metal trash can with her right foot as she turned to hustle out of the gym. It clattered across the floor with a racket that echoed through the cavernous facility.

Kaylee froze. Ellison froze. Alana froze. Then Kaylee heard Alana curse, though Alana and Ellison had to be a hundred feet away.

Well then. No chance to flee. Instead, Kaylee did the only thing she could to still maintain some personal dignity. She started across the gym toward Alana and Ellison. At the same time, Alana and Ellison stepped toward her. They met up somewhere near the bank of twenty elliptical machines.

"Hi," Alana said.

"Hi," Kaylee replied, her voice stiff. "I didn't expect that anyone would be here."

"We're ... training. I've been training Alana for a while now," Ellison told Kaylee.

"I can see that. I was going to work out too. But I think maybe we need to talk, Alana. Don't you?" Kaylee suggested.

Alana nodded and turned to Ellison. "Let me talk with Kaylee. If I have time, I'll come back and finish up."

"Sounds good. I'm going to do my pecs," Ellison responded. He didn't wait for the girls to say good-bye, he just jogged off toward the rear of the gym.

"So," Alana said. "You're turning into a gym rat."

"Not funny."

"So yeah. I'm training with Ellison. How much did you see?"

Kaylee didn't answer with words. Instead, her lips formed an exaggerated pucker.

"Okay. So you saw."

"I saw."

"We like each other. What can I tell you?" Alana said defensively.

"I thought you liked Cory. I was helping you to like Cory. Or to get Cory to like you. Or something like that."

"I do like Cory," Alana told her. "Stand by."

There was a water cooler to her right. Alana went to it and filled a paper cup with cold water, then came back to Kaylee. "But Cory's not so into me. Why, I don't know. But that's the fact. Meanwhile, Ellison is a great guy, right? Right?"

Kaylee had to nod. Yes. Ellison was a good guy. He was maybe the smartest guy she'd ever met in her life. And for a smart guy to be in a body like his with looks like his? Well, that seemed unfair to the rest of the male half of the species. And she knew more about Cory's feelings than Alana did. It wasn't just that Cory wasn't into Alana. It was that he was interested in Kaylee.

"Yeah. He's cool. But …"

"What?" Alana pressed.

"I just think you have to be straight up with Cory. And tell him what's going on," Kaylee said.

"Okay," Alana promised, then downed the water. "You're right. I will. Anything else?"

Kaylee's heart pounded. Here she was, demanding honesty from Alana, while there was something she was hiding herself. It wasn't right for her to hide it. No matter what might happen if she shared it. No matter whether Alana talked to Cory first or not.

"Yeah," Kaylee said. "There is one more thing."

"What's that? And then I'll go finish my training." Alana's mood had turned happy. "Three days to the wedding, you know. I have to look great."

"You may not like this …"

"What?"

Kaylee steeled herself. "Well, if you're with Ellison, I guess it's not a problem. I think Cory and I like each other. A lot. Like, a lot." She looked at Alana, who stared at her.

Then Alana smiled. "Good luck with him," she said softly. "He's an awesome guy. You should be with an awesome guy."

"You're not … you're not mad?" Kaylee asked, astonished.

"Mad? About what? That you told me? I'd be mad if you hadn't told me!"

"Great!" Kaylee exclaimed. She hugged Alana. She felt Alana hug her back. She'd just gotten the green light she'd wanted. She didn't know what was going to happen with him, but at least there was nothing now in the way of what *could* happen. The gates to a Kaylee-and-Cory relationship were officially open.

CHAPTER TWELVE

"She told me that it was fine that you and I are seeing each other," Cory reported as he threaded his expensive sports car through the thick Thursday afternoon traffic on Las Vegas Boulevard. Weekends were always big in Vegas, but people flew in early to extend their vacations. By that night, the city would be almost as crowded as a Friday or Saturday night.

Kaylee pushed her seat back a little to give herself more legroom. "She said basically the same thing to me."

"So I guess we're good to see where this goes."

Kaylee smiled warmly. "I guess so."

It was the day after Kaylee had walked in on Alana kissing Ellison in the gym. True to her word, Alana had talked to Cory. In fact, Cory related that Alana had come to him that same morning. They'd had coffee together at Caffeine Central. She'd apologized for not being clearer about what was going on with her and Ellison and wished him well. She even wished him well with Kaylee, if that was what he wanted. She hoped that they could continue to be friends. She promised to do nothing to hurt their friendship and hoped that he would do the same.

Cory and Kaylee had been assigned the job of delivering some last-minute wedding invitations to various people around town. Abra, the wedding planner, didn't trust Federal Express or a regular courier service. Cory drove while Kaylee navigated with the GPS on her phone, even though Cory knew the city better than anyone.

Kaylee was about to tell Cory to turn right when yet another text came in from Reavis. He'd been texting her every four hours for two days.

"Anything new?"

"Turn right. It's from Reavis," she told Cory, who turned off the Strip and headed south on Tropicana. "He wants to know if there's anything new."

"Like you wouldn't call him if you heard something," Cory said.

Cory was right, Kaylee thought. Reavis had to know that Kaylee would call immediately with any news about him getting a Teen Tower gig or not.

"I know. I wonder if Steve isn't going to decide until after the wedding."

"He may not decide at all," Cory said.

"That's crazy."

"That's Vegas, and that's showbiz," Cory corrected. "I know Steve. He could sit on this for a week, a month, or even longer." He slowed the car for a red light.

"What should I text back, then?" Kaylee asked.

"Just the truth. No news. Stand by. Don't do anything to hurt himself."

Kaylee tried to keep it short and sweet.

"Nothing yet. Still hopeful. Stay cool."

A moment later, Reavis texted back a quick, **"KK."**

"It has to suck to be a performer," she said softly.

"Why do you say that?"

"Because your whole life depends on what other people think of you."

"Kaylee?"

"Yeah?"

Cory adjusted the car's sun visor. "Don't kid yourself. It's not just performers like Reavis. Everyone's life depends on what other people think of them."

Kaylee thought about that for a moment. It was sort of true. If travelers soured on a particular hotel, the hotel lost business. If a brand of car got a bad reputation, no one would buy it. It wasn't just performers. It was everyone. It was the law of the human jungle.

Her cell sounded with a call, not a text. She thought it would be Reavis, but she didn't recognize the incoming number.

"Hello?" she answered.

"Hey, Kaylee baby. It's Al at the front desk at the Apache."

Al? Why would he be calling her? Al had no reason to call unless there was a problem. If there was a problem, that problem had to be with either one of two people. Reavis, potentially. But more likely, Aunt Karen. Ugh.

"Yes?" she said hesitantly.

"Uh, hate to do this to you," Al's New York-tinged voice rang through the phone. "But we've got a bit of a situation here."

Her heart quickened. "What kind of a situation?"

"We got the ambulance, the paramedics, the whole nine yards. They're in your aunt's room."

"How is she?" Kaylee demanded, heartsick and worried. "Is she alive? Please tell me she's alive!"

"She's alive," Al acknowledged. "But not in great shape. Drugs, they say."

"We're on our way."

"Don't bother. They're taking her to University Medical Center. Go there," Al instructed.

"Okay. Thanks." Kaylee clicked off and turned to Cory, who was looking at her with great concern. "Problem with my aunt. Drug overdose. UMC. Now, please!"

Kaylee had been in hospitals like UMC before. In fact, they were the only kind of hospital she'd ever visited. Not the fancy hospitals where people with good insurance went, but the public ones that had to take everyone who came through the door and treat every case. When her grandmother had been in the worst of her dementia, before she was put into the long-term care facility, Kaylee found herself at the county hospital nearly every week because her grandmother would wander away from home, get lost, and be brought in by the police for a mandatory psychiatric evaluation.

The main waiting room was depressing. Lots of security and lots of families—many of them non-English speakers—with a banged-up floor, plastic chairs scattered around, and a few potted plants. The noise was unbelievable, the smell a mix of antiseptic floor wash and unwashed bodies, and the fluorescent lighting harsh and unflattering. This is where Kaylee and Cory were told to wait for the doctor to come out to see them. In the emergency room, they'd been given a little number on a stand, like the kind that some restaurants would give out so that the servers would know where to bring meal orders.

At least Karen was alive, Kaylee thought as she sent another text to Alana explaining the situation. Alana texted back not to worry, that as long as the invitations were delivered by dinnertime, they'd be fine. Since it was just two o'clock, Kaylee relaxed a little. She did worry some about the quality of care that Karen would be getting. County hospitals had doctors and nurses who tried valiantly but were overworked and underpaid. It wasn't the kind of job that a medical professional would take if he or she could possibly avoid it.

They'd been there for an hour already. The emergency room doctors said that Karen's life was not in danger, but that she'd clearly overdosed on something. Kaylee and Cory would have to wait for a toxicology report to get all the details.

After an hour and a half, an female Indian doctor in green scrubs approached them, a clipboard in her hands. "Kaylee Ryan?"

Kaylee stood. So did Cory. "I'm Kaylee."

"I'm Doctor Gupta. I'm taking care of your aunt."

"How is she?" Kaylee asked.

"There's a history of drug use with her, correct?"

Kaylee nodded. "Yes, unfortunately. Mostly meth, I think. But she's been clean for a while. Until today, that is."

The doctor shook her head. "She hasn't been clean. She's just changed what she's using. We brought her in with an OD on heroin."

"Heroin?" Kaylee screeched. "Heroin? Karen doesn't use heroin!"

"Toxicology doesn't lie. Anyway, she's sedated. I don't know how long we're going to keep her. I want to test for Hepatitis C and a few other things. We've got some beds open. I think the best thing to do is to hold her for a day or two."

"Can I see her?" Kaylee asked.

Dr. Gupta shook her head. "Not now. Later, if you want to wait. We'll let you know."

"How much later?" Kaylee pressed.

"At least an hour. Maybe more."

Kaylee took a deep breath. Okay. An hour wasn't going to make a difference. At least her aunt wasn't going to die.

"What do you want to do?" Cory asked her.

"Stay and see her, then we can go."

Dr. Gupta fidgeted a little. "Well, I'm very busy. I need to get back to work. Here's a card with the nurse's station number on it." She handed Kaylee a business card. "Let them know what you want to do. Just leave the number card here. Someone will pick it up."

Without a formal good-bye, Dr. Gupta strode away in search of other people waiting for updates. Kaylee watched her, wondering idly what the doctor's life was like and thinking about all the things that she must see in the course of an average day. It couldn't be easy dealing with cases like Aunt Karen. It had to be really depressing.

"So, we stay," Kaylee said.

"I'm in," Cory assured her.

Kaylee sighed. "Can we get some food or something?"

There was a Quick-Mart directly across the street from the hospital. Kaylee called the nurses' station, told the receptionist that she'd be back in forty-five minutes, and left her cell number in case of an emergency. Then she and Cory walked across the street. Like so many Nevada stores, the Quick-Mart had a few slot machines. While Cory wandered around looking for food that wasn't full of chemicals and preservatives, Kaylee found herself drawn to the slots. No one was using them. She felt around in her pocket. She had some quarters. God. She knew how much better she would feel if she could play for a few minutes. Even one minute. Just one minute of play and the stress of the afternoon could be balanced out.

Kaylee did a quick scan for Cory. He was over by the slushy machine, preoccupied with choosing munchies. He wouldn't see. And the elderly clerk was busy with customers. He wouldn't stop her.

She dug for the quarters and went to the slot machine.

"Hey!" the clerk growled. "What are you doing?"

Oh no.

Kaylee stammered out some kind of embarrassed response. Her face flushed. Hot blood pounded in her ears. Then Cory was next to her.

"I agree," he said softly. "What are you doing?"

Kaylee looked at the clerk, then to Cory, then to the slot machine, and then back to Cory.

"I don't know what I'm doing, Cory," she confessed. "I really don't know."

CHAPTER THIRTEEN

There was a small grassy area with playground equipment on the hospital grounds. It was more of a place for visiting families to sit and let their kids goof around for a while than an official park. It had a merry-go-round, swings, see-saw, monkey bars, and a sandpit for toddlers, plus some scattered benches. This was where Cory brought Kaylee after he discovered her staring longingly at the slots. Kaylee had moved mutely as Cory walked her over to the cash register where he purchased a couple bottles of water, two bananas, a pre-packaged cheese sandwich, and a small bag of trail mix. "I'd get a couple of Snickers, but they'd melt before we could eat them," he joked.

Kaylee tried to force a smile, but it didn't come. She

felt terrible that Cory had caught her longing to gamble. That terrible feeling was piled on top of the helplessness of having her only relative in the hospital. She felt weak, confused, and small. Fortunately, Cory didn't say anything more until they got to the deserted playground. There, he sat them down, opened one of the bottles of water, and handed it to her.

"I just want to say," he began, "that whatever was happening in there with you and those slot machines? It's nothing compared to what happened to me at Stanford."

Kaylee nodded. Cory had shared with her the story of his depression when he went away to college. "You mean when you couldn't get out of bed in the morning."

"I mean when I couldn't brush my teeth, wash my hair, get dressed, or even go to the cafeteria for breakfast," he agreed. "I missed classes, I didn't shower, and I was a total mess. You're a long way from that. Compared to me? You're in great shape."

"Thank you, Doctor P," Kaylee managed a joke.

"You're welcome." Cory drank some of the water and opened the package of trail mix. "So, what just happened in there? Has it happened before?"

For a moment, Kaylee thought about fibbing. It would save face. Then she decided not to lie. He was right. She was functioning and even thriving, by any objective measure. She wasn't one of those ladies who sat at the slot machine at 6:45 a.m., having been there all night.

No, you're not, she heard the voice in her head say. *Not yet. But who's to say you couldn't turn into one of them?*

She ran her tongue over the roof of her mouth, trying to think of how to explain it. There wasn't any way that didn't make her look bad. "I can't really explain it," she told him, thinking back to her arrival in Vegas and seeing a woman play slots in the lobby of the Apache Motel. She recalled how exciting that had been. "From the first time I saw someone play, I liked it. But I didn't just like it in my head. I liked it in my heart. It made me feel good in a way I've never felt before."

"I've heard of that," Cory commented. "That doesn't happen with me. I can take it or leave it. But I've heard people talk about gambling that way."

Now that she'd begun to speak, it was easier. "The first time I played a slot machine was at the Apache Motel. I was upset about something. Al—he's the boss there—let me play. I felt better afterward. It happened a few times, actually."

"So … what was it like when we were playing blackjack at the warehouse casino?" Cory asked.

She smiled a little. "I liked who I was playing next to, that's for sure."

"I liked who I was next to too. But what about the experience?"

She closed her eyes for a moment and thought back. "Honestly? I could have stayed there until they closed. I could have stayed all night. I could have stayed even if I was the only one left in the building."

Cory touched her arm. "You and a lot of other people. Gambling can be addictive. It can pull you in like a moth to a flame."

Kaylee had a sudden memory of her various walks past the casino at the LV Skye. She recalled standing outside the casino looking in, hoping that the security guards might turn away so she could slip inside. Not to gamble. She was underage and didn't want to be arrested. Just to breathe the air, hear the sounds, and be close to the tables and the action.

Yeah, she thought. *Like a moth drawn to a flame. Or a star sucked in by a black hole.*

"I know what that feels like," she confessed.

"And we're here because your aunt can't stay away from drugs," Cory noted. A courageous squirrel approached them. Cory tossed it a few nuts. The squirrel grabbed the biggest one and scurried away to eat it.

"Are you saying I'm addicted to gambling?" Kaylee asked, shocked at the thought.

Cory shrugged and made a face. "I'm just a guy who had a problem with depression. I don't know."

The more she considered it, the idea of being addicted to gambling wasn't so shocking. Her aunt was definitely an addict. Her mother drank a lot. Their DNA was in her genes. If addiction could be passed from generation to generation, then maybe it got passed to her.

"It could be in my genes, though," Kaylee realized. "Which means if I don't want to wreck my life, I have to stop."

Cory threw a few more nuts to the squirrel. "I think that would be a good idea."

"I think it would be a *great* idea," Kaylee declared. She did not want to end up like Karen. No way. "I need to stay away from slots and stay away from casinos. Even the no-money one at Teen Tower."

"Or else I'll chuck you in a Champagne fountain," Cory mock-threatened.

Kaylee laughed for the first time in a long time. Her first night in Vegas, she'd been shoved into a Champagne fountain at Alana's eighteenth birthday party. It was how she'd met Alana. That had been good fortune that she couldn't control. Going into a casino or playing slots was something she could control. Sure, she'd been attracted to slot machines and casinos. But she thought about all the times she'd passed slot machines and *didn't* play, and the nights she *hadn't* gone back to the warehouse casino. She could do this. She knew she could.

"Deal," she told Cory.

Her cell sounded with an incoming call. She didn't recognize the number.

"Hello?" she answered.

"Is this Kaylee Ryan?"

"I'm Kaylee."

"This is the nurses' station on the third floor. Your aunt is sleeping, but if you want, you can see her."

Kaylee went upstairs alone. Cory wasn't authorized since he wasn't immediate family. A Filipina nurse walked her to Karen's room. She was the only patient in a room for two people and was hooked up to an IV, with other monitors attached to her fingers and chest. She looked ravaged. Tired. Old. And out like a light.

"Stay as long as you want," the nurse told Kaylee. "She's not waking up anytime soon."

The nurse departed. Kaylee was alone with her aunt. What to do? What to say? Karen couldn't hear her anyway. For a moment, Kaylee thought about leaving. Then she decided to voice the words that were in her heart. There was one of the hospital's crappy plastic chairs by her aunt's bedside. She pulled it closer to her aunt and sat.

"Well," she said softly. "Hi, Aunt Karen. It's me, Kaylee. You can't hear me, and it's probably good that you can't. I don't know what's going on in your soul, Karen. I know you've had a hard life. But a lot of people have had hard lives. I know you've got demons in you. No one wants to end up in the hospital with an IV in their arm after overdosing on heroin.

"A lot of us have demons. I'm trying to make a new life for myself, Karen. Do you understand what you're doing to that life? How hard you're making it for me? How I feel like I'm responsible for you when you're twenty-five years older than I am? How crazy is that?"

Kaylee took a deep breath and thought about the future. "Here's what I want, Karen. I want you to do two things. I want you to get well and get your life together. I really do. It's why I helped you at the Apache Motel, and why I would help you again. But I also want you to help me. If there are going to be more disasters, and more evictions, and more running away, and more overdoses, and more ambulances? I want you to think about how that's going to affect me as well as you. Because those things do affect me.

"If you're going to wreck your life more? Please, Aunt

Karen. I'm begging you. Find a way to leave me out of it. Okay?"

Kaylee found herself weeping. It was heartbreaking to say those words. Karen was all the family she had left. It killed her inside to say to her aunt that she was a lesion on Kaylee's life. But her conversation with Cory had pointed out one big black hole she needed to avoid. She didn't need a second one.

"We'll talk when you wake up, okay, Aunt Karen?" Kaylee got the words out between her tears. Then she kissed her on the forehead and left the room.

CHAPTER FOURTEEN

The next day, the day of the rehearsal dinner, Kaylee kept waiting to hear from Karen in the hospital. She expected the call where Karen announced she had been discharged and was going to return to room 109 at the Apache. Then she expected that Karen was going to ask her for more help, which Kaylee was reluctant to give.

That call never came. As the day went on, Kaylee got worried. That's why she phoned the third floor of the hospital in the late afternoon and asked the nurse who answered how her aunt was doing. "Karen Clarke, can you give me an update?"

"She's gone," the nurse reported after Kaylee identified herself.

Kaylee misinterpreted. "Gone? She died?!"

"No, no," the nurse said. "She's very much alive. But she checked out around noontime. Against medical advice, by the way. That's all I've got. Thank you for calling."

The nurse hung up. Kaylee was shocked. "Against medical advice" meant that Karen had left the hospital even though the doctors hadn't discharged her. What would have provoked that kind of behavior? She called her aunt's cell, but Karen didn't answer, so she left a message for her aunt to return the call. That call came in while Kaylee was doing a sweep through the noisy game room. She missed the call, but her aunt did leave a very pointed message on Kaylee's voice mail.

"Hey, babe, it's your aunt. I'm outta the hospital and outta here. Wouldn't want to be the one to destroy the life of my only niece, after all. Thanks for nothing. Oh! Guess what? I was awake when you were in my room yesterday. I heard everything you said. Every single little word. Thanks for the kiss on the forehead. That was sooooooo sweet. Bye. Don't call me back."

Kaylee listened to it twice and deleted it. But she couldn't delete the sick feeling in her stomach that lingered like a stain of vomit on a rug. Karen had heard everything she'd said. Her aunt had to think she was the worst person in the universe. Kaylee didn't believe she was, but her belief didn't make her feel any better.

Later that afternoon, Kaylee went to Alana to tell her about the call from Karen. She thought about texting a warning to say she was coming, but she figured it was just as easy to go up to the penthouse where Alana would be prepping for the rehearsal dinner at Mondrian, the nicest restaurant in the LV Skye complex. It would only take a few minutes anyway. The elevator operator took her right to the top and opened directly into the penthouse. Mr. Clermont, the butler, was on duty in the hallway when she arrived. As usual, he wore his tuxedo and a bow tie. He actually smiled a bit when he saw her.

"The estimable Miss Kaylee Ryan," he intoned. "Making an unexpected and unannounced visit. How may I help you?"

"Is Alana here?" Kaylee asked.

He nodded. "She is, indeed. In her room with young Miss Gold-Blum and young Miss Walker, who are acting as dressers, makeup artists, and critics-in-chief as Miss Alana prepares for the rehearsal dinner. Are you here to participate in the festivities?"

Kaylee grinned at his good humor. Mr. Clermont had never shown any personality to her before this moment.

She liked it. And it was no shocker that Alana was with Zoey and Chalice either.

"I haven't been invited to the party, but I do need to talk to Alana," Kaylee told him.

"Oh? Well then, in that case follow me."

Mr. Clermont led the way through the penthouse to Alana's room. He asked Kaylee to wait at the end of the hallway while he knocked on Alana's closed door. Kaylee could discern muffled voices and music from the other side as he approached and knocked. Then she heard Alana ask who it was.

"Mr. Clermont. Two things, Miss Alana," he intoned. "Thirty minutes until you're due at Mondrian. And Miss Kaylee is here to see you. She said she knows it's unexpected, but it's important."

Alana called back through the open door. "Show her in, Mr. Clermont."

Mr. Clermont turned and motioned to Kaylee. "Your entry has been granted, proceed at your own peril," he said.

Kaylee approached, whispered a thank you to the butler, and then entered Alana's room. Alana stood between Zoey and Chalice. She was wearing a golden yellow sleeveless dress and black shoes. Her lustrous hair had been brushed out. She wore foundation on her face, but not the final touches of what Kaylee was sure would be a careful makeup job. She looked wonderful in the dress. Those training sessions with Ellison had certainly helped.

"Great dress," Kaylee said. "Hi, Zoey. Hi, Chalice."

"Hi," Chalice said with a warm wave.

Zoey didn't respond. Kaylee didn't press the moment. If she was ever going to make friends with Zoey Gold-Blum—a highly unlikely prospect—it was not going to be in Alana's room thirty minutes before Alana was to go to the rehearsal dinner. For a moment, though, Kaylee did feel bad that she hadn't been invited to help out with Alana's prep for the Mondrian dinner. But since the wedding had been announced, except for official business and that surprise meeting in the gym, they'd barely seen each other.

Alana took a couple of steps toward her. "Actually, I'm glad you're here. I've got news for you."

"I've got news for you too. Can I tell you privately?" What she had to say was far too personal to share in front of Zoey, though she didn't mind if Chalice heard it. Zoey, though? She could just imagine what Zoey would say about her aunt being taken to the hospital in an ambulance. It was sort of a miracle it hadn't already made the *Stripped* blog.

"Hey, you're with friends," Zoey called out sarcastically.

Kaylee stood helplessly, looking to Alana for direction.

Finally, Alana nodded and motioned that they could talk outside the room. Alana left the room first. Kaylee saw Zoey offer a contemptuous little wave as she followed Alana out.

Once the door was closed, Alana turned to Kaylee with something close to impatience. "I don't have a lot of time, and you know why. What's up?" she asked.

Kaylee got right to it. "It's about my aunt. The one who OD'd."

"The one in the hospital?"

Kaylee nodded. "Yep. But she isn't in the hospital anymore. She left town. And she said it was my fault."

Kaylee started to weep. Her tears were as heartfelt as they were unexpected. It felt like she was crying not just for her aunt, but for all the love and constancy from adults she always wished for but never had. All her life, the only person that Kaylee could safely rely on was herself. For a time, she had thought that she might be able to rely on Alana. But the last week had shown her that thought was based on hopes and dreams instead of on reality. Alana hadn't even told her that she was hanging out with Ellison. She'd been the last one to know.

The moment reminded her of an old country song that her grandmother had sung around the double-wide trailer, back when her grandmother could still remember song lyrics. "The last one to know," she'd croon, "is the first one to cry."

She noticed that Alana stood there uncomfortably, instead of embracing her like a real friend might. Was it because she didn't want to mess up her makeup, or was it because Alana didn't really want to be there at all? There was no way to know without asking, and Kaylee was not about to pose that question.

"What happened to her?" Alana asked her.

Kaylee gritted her teeth and told the story of what had happened in the hospital, the phone call from Karen, and the aftermath.

"I was mean," she told Alana. "I was horrible. I told her she couldn't ruin my life anymore."

"That doesn't sound mean. That sounds honest."

"I guess," Kaylee muttered. "But it still hurts."

Finally, Alana embraced her gingerly. Kaylee was grateful to be in her arms. She'd thought Alana would understand. And it seemed now that Alana did understand. The open question was how much Alana cared.

"Okay," Kaylee said. She stepped away from the embrace, settled herself, and wiped some lingering tears from her eyes. "I know you've got the dinner. I just wanted to tell you in person. I won't have to miss any more work because of Karen. Sorry to bother you."

"It's fine," Alana declared.

Kaylee shook her head. "Actually, it isn't fine. But it is the way it is. Have fun tonight. I'll see you at the reception tomorrow. And you really do look great. What did you want to talk to me about?"

Alana shook her head. Time was getting tight. "It can wait. Bye."

Kaylee retraced her steps to where Mr. Clermont stood again by the elevator. Wordlessly, he handed her a tissue.

"Did you hear me with Alana?"

He shook his head. "No. I didn't hear you. And if I did, I wouldn't tell you. A butler's job is first to be discreet, and then to do everything else."

She dried her eyes. "Thank you, Mr. Clermont."

"You're welcome, Miss Kaylee," Mr. Clermont said. "If it matters at all what I think, Miss Kaylee, I'm rooting for you."

"Know what I want to do?" Kaylee asked Cory.

"Gamble?" he responded.

"Not funny," she told him. "Well, actually it is funny, but it's not funny. But you know what I mean."

He raised a finger. "How about crash the rehearsal dinner? It's a lot better food than we just had."

Kaylee laughed. It felt great to be with Cory after that

weird face-to-face with Alana up in the penthouse. They'd stayed at Teen Tower until eight o'clock when things there wound down. Then Cory had proposed a low-rent dinner at his favorite fast-food joint, which Kaylee had never heard of, Bachi Burger, out on Sahara Avenue far north of town. Bachi offered Asian-tinged barbecued burgers, and Kaylee had eaten two of them plus a vanilla shake.

Afterward, Cory had proposed that they go out to Las Vegas's last remaining drive-in movie theater. Kaylee checked the movie times on her phone. They'd missed the last showing by about fifteen minutes. She wasn't all that upset, though. She knew what guys and girls who liked each other did in cars at drive-ins, and she wasn't sure she was ready to do that with Cory. Not yet anyway.

"I've got an idea," Kaylee said. "How about we go to the top of Stratosphere?"

"Interesting. Are you in the mood to barf?"

"I have a strong stomach. Besides, by the time we get there, we'll have digested. Come on. It'll be fun."

Stratosphere was a casino-hotel at the east end of the Strip. Its main claim to fame was the big tower that went almost a thousand feet in the sky above the city, sort of like Las Vegas's version of a space needle. Kaylee had read that in the tower were various nightclubs and attractions as well as a bunch of death-defying amusement park-like rides that flung the passengers out over the city. She loved theme park roller-coasters. They were a way to be scared when she was still absolutely safe. The rides at Stratosphere sounded horribly scary.

"Stratosphere is a tourist trap!" Cory protested.

"Great. Let's act like we're tourists." She looked at him and batted her eyelashes as obviously as she dared. "You're not going to say no to me, are you?"

"No. Just don't hurl on me."

They laughed. He started the car and drove all the way back to town and then north to Stratosphere. There, he paid the admission fee, and they joined a big group of tourists in the elevator to the top of the tower. Once off the elevator, Kaylee went straight to the Insanity ride, which was nine-hundred feet above the street. The ride featured a huge arm that pushed riders in an open-air car more than twenty yards from the building and spun them in all directions. At one point, they were pointed straight down to the ground.

Kaylee was pleased to hear Cory scream longer and harder than she did. She was even more pleased when he refused to go a second time.

"I'll watch you," he said, looking a little pale.

Kaylee did it again. And then, just to spite him, she did it one more time. She rode all the other Stratosphere attractions too. Cory was content to take pictures. It was fun. Just pure fun with a guy she liked and in an emotional place where nothing could go wrong. She wished that life could be like that all the time.

CHAPTER FIFTEEN

"Omigosh! Kaylee! You look fantastic!"

Kaylee, who had been standing uncertainly outside the Desert Ballroom while waiting for Cory to join her, turned around. For the last fifteen minutes, well-dressed wedding guests had been having their electronic credentials checked by a small army of security people. The party was black-and-white themed. The guys were all in tuxedos, while the women wore formal dresses of varying lengths.

Kaylee had paid a visit to the mall. She had splurged on a gorgeous BCBG dress. It was the nicest outfit she'd ever owned. She'd also purchased no-name strappy black satin sandals. She'd borrowed a black patent-leather Prada clutch from Chalice to match.

She grinned when she saw who was calling to her.

Chalice pushed through the crowd. She had on the slinkiest black cocktail dress Kaylee had ever seen. The dress plunged with a V-shaped slit between her impressive breasts, with black-and-white patterned four-inch heels. Her curly red hair was tamed into a perfect chignon. It was a classic counterpoint to her amazing dress. She looked both sexy and beautiful.

"Hi, Chalice," Kaylee greeted her with a makeup-preserving gentle hug. "You look great too."

"Thanks. I don't know why people don't get dressed up more often," Chalice told her. "The whole world looks better."

"Because most people can't afford these kinds of clothes," Kaylee said.

"Hey, you kept to your small budget, and you borrowed the bag, which looks great," Chalice pointed out. "You still look like a million bucks. What did you end up doing for a wedding present?"

Kaylee sighed. The issue of the present had been a big problem for her. There was nothing she could afford that wouldn't have seemed stupid. "I made a donation to Children's Hospital in their honor," she said. "I hope that's okay."

"It's more than okay," Chalice assured her. "Way better than a crystal bowl."

Zoey materialized out of the crowd. She had on a white silk dress and white pumps, plus a stunning silver necklace. "Hey, look. It's the Odd Couple! Are you two lovers yet?"

Kaylee frowned at her. "Why are you being like this? It's a wedding. Can't we all just have a good time?"

"I was having a good time until I saw my best friend hanging out with the girl I'm going to have to work with. Unfortunately," Zoey said with a sniff.

"What are you talking about? 'Going to have to work with?' " Kaylee asked with venom in her voice. She didn't usually get aggressive with other people, but Zoey was just so … hateful. "Last time I checked, you work for Alana and me. Not *with* me."

Zoey did the world's slowest headshake. "Nope. Things have changed. Check with Alana. You and I? We're now co-assistants. Hey, you know what they say? Change is good."

What the hell? Since when did Alana promote Zoey? And if she had made Zoey her co-assistant, why was Zoey telling her this and not Alana? It made Kaylee mad. There was just so much that any person could take. She literally bit her own tongue so she wouldn't say something that she would later regret.

Chalice looked up at Zoey. "You weren't supposed to

be the one to tell her," she chided. "Alana wanted to tell Kaylee herself."

"Oh, come on, Chalice, relax. What's done is done. Kaylee's a big girl. She can take some bad news. Can't you, Kaylee?"

Kaylee's eyes narrowed. "I'm not going to answer that."

"No? Too bad. Because I have a feeling there's going to be more bad news coming soon. Like …" Zoey faked a thoughtful attitude. "Oh! I know. Like you not having a job at Teen Tower at all."

Chalice stepped between them. "Zoey? You know that's not true. And if it was true, the whole town knows what a great job Kaylee has done here. My dad will get her on at the Wynn, or Aria, or Vdara, the Bellagio, Caesars, or anywhere else she wants to work." Her voice softened so much that it was hard to hear amid the hubbub of the crowd heading into the ballroom. "Kaylee, I promise. You don't have to worry."

Zoey frowned and shrugged her shoulders. "I guess that settles it. I'll see the Odd Couple inside." She flounced off. Kaylee could feel the disdain.

"Whoa," Kaylee said.

Chalice smiled. "Classic Zoey. If she's with you, she's with you. If she's against you, watch out. Actually, I should be more worried about her than you."

"What about what she said about working with me? Is it true?"

Chalice seemed to hesitate.

"What?"

"Alana told us not to say anything to you."

"Oh well," Kaylee said more lightly than she felt. She'd see Alana in the ballroom. If she had a chance to ask her about it, she would. If not, it would have to wait for tomorrow. In the meantime, where was Cory? She scanned the crowd for him …

And there he was in an elegant tuxedo with a quirky broad bow tie and cummerbund. He spotted her at about the same time that she saw him. They waved at the same time too. He grinned. She grinned. When he came to her and embraced her, then Chalice, and then her again, she forgot all about Zoey Gold-Blum.

"Come on," he told Kaylee and Chalice. He put both hands on his hips. Chalice took one arm; Kaylee took the other. "Two gorgeous ladies and little ol' me. Let's make an entrance."

It was a wedding reception like no other. The ballroom had scores of big round tables, like at an awards show. There was a dance band on the stage playing swing tunes as people entered. The decorations were in the same black-and-white colors that the guests had all been asked to wear, with centerpieces of black-and-white quartz and white roses, and marvelous shaped ribbons and silk fabric hanging down the walls. As at Alana's birthday party a few weeks before, there was a Champagne fountain. Kaylee also walked through an area of massive black-and-white spray-painted ice sculptures, plus an actual art gallery of black-and-white paintings by such luminaries as Georgia O'Keeffe and Franz Kline, as well as black-and-white photographs by renowned photographers like Alfred Stieglitz and Ansel Adams.

The entertainment began from the moment the crowd was seated. One star after another: Garth Brooks, Brad Paisley, Kelly Clarkson, Beyoncé, Ziggy Marley, and more. During the meal, there were speeches and roasts of the happy couple by comedians young and old. Louis C.K. brought the house down with a routine about why Roxanne had been so courageous to go out with Steve in the first place—how he himself would never go out with Steve Skye.

When Jay Z took over as master of ceremonies, he got Roxanne to dance with him onstage. Dinner was incredible: a menu prepared by Jean-Claude Chanderot, who was going to open the LV Skye's second four-star restaurant. Kaylee, Cory, and Chalice had been seated at a table with Ellison, Zoey, and several others whom Kaylee didn't know. Zoey busied herself talking to Ellison, which meant she didn't focus on Kaylee for a while. As for Alana, Kaylee saw her at the head table with the rest of the wedding party. She realized that there wasn't going to be much of a chance to talk tonight. Not about Zoey, not about Reavis—there was still no word on whether he was going to be offered a gig at Teen Tower—not about anything. Whatever. Their conversation could wait until the next day.

Actually, as Kaylee learned soon enough, the conversation didn't have to wait. Between the end of the main meal and service of the first dessert—the second dessert would be the wedding cake, which would be cut and served near the end of the party—while Kanye West was performing, Kaylee's cell sounded with an incoming text. To her surprise, it was Alana.

"Hi. Meet me by bubbly."

Kaylee actually laughed since a Champagne fountain played such a big role in their history. She answered sassily.

"U gonna push me in again?"

"Ha! Just meet me," Alana replied.

Kaylee excused herself from the table and hurried to the fountain. As Alana approached, she grabbed two crystal goblets from a passing waiter. She handed one to Kaylee.

"It's just water," Alana said. "How about a toast to the happy couple?"

Kaylee raised her glass. "To you and Ellison?"

Alana laughed. "That's not what I had in mind. But sure, why not?"

They drank.

"I can't stay long, but there's something I want you to know," Alana shared.

"About Zoey being another assistant? She already told me."

Alana raised her eyebrows. "Really?"

"No, Alana. I'm making it up. Of course really."

Alana sighed. "I deserved that. Okay. I'm sorry. You should have heard it from me first."

"It's true?"

"Yeah, it's true," Alana nodded. "She's been great this week. I think I could use two assistants. It'll be fine."

Kaylee took this in and remembered what Chalice had said before they came into the reception. It made her feel bold. "Hey. It's your call. But I'm telling you—if she treats me badly? There's only so much I can take. If it's too much, I'm outta here. Nothing is worth being abused for."

"Duly noted," Alana said drily.

"I mean it," Kaylee declared, more confident by the moment. "And you'll miss me."

"Relax, Kaylee," Alana told her. "It'll be fine."

"It's going to snow tomorrow too," Kaylee cracked.

Alana laughed. Then Kaylee laughed too. For the moment, anyway, the problem with Zoey was defused. It wasn't going away, but it wasn't going to explode either.

"Is that all you wanted to tell me?" Kaylee asked. "Because this is kind of a weird time."

Alana shook her head. "No. There's something else. It's about your aunt. I found out why she left town."

"Oh?"

"And I can predict with full confidence that she'll never come back. It isn't in her best interest to come back. And it is in her best interest to stay far away from Vegas."

Kaylee raised her eyebrows. "What's that supposed to mean?"

"It means my dad wants you to be able to do your job without worrying about her, which is pretty funny considering that you're talking about quitting," Alana told her. "Nice dress, by the way."

"Thanks about the dress. Clueless about your dad and my aunt."

"Okay. Here's the thing." Alana looked each way, as if to be sure that no one was listening. "He told me that he paid her to leave. And he's paying her to stay away."

"What?! That's ... that's crazy!" Kaylee sputtered.

"Nope. It's just my dad," Alana said. "And ... holy moly. Look at that!"

Alana pointed to the stage. Her father stood center stage with a mic. Behind him was a backdrop of a man in a mask. Across the backdrop was the word "PHANTOM" superimposed in big block letters.

"Ladies and gentlemen! For your entertainment tonight in anticipation of his new gig at Teen Tower, the LV Skye presents the hottest magician and escape artist in town, the young man the whole city is buzzing about ... Phantom!"

Oh. My. God. Kaylee's knees weakened at this electrifying surprise, but joy filled her heart as Reavis came out on stage. He was greeted by thunderous applause from the wedding guests. Then he performed a fantastic routine with a female assistant that Kaylee didn't know, culminating with a physics-defying levitation illusion where he somehow seemed to float up and over the audience.

"Did you know anything about this?" Kaylee demanded.

Alana shook her head. "Like you said before, clueless."

Reavis finished to a standing ovation. The band started to play. Roxanne took the mic from Steve and implored everyone to come and dance. Alana and Kaylee looked at each other awkwardly. The logical people for them to dance with were Ellison and Cory. Alana with Ellison and Kaylee with Cory. But Kaylee used to like Ellison, and Alana used to like Cory. Now they'd switched.

"You heard my stepmother. Shall we?" Alana asked.

"You're the new stepdaughter, it's your call." Kaylee tossed the decision back to Alana.

"Oh, hell. I want to stay on my dad's good side. Let's do it."

They moved toward the dance floor. Cory met Kaylee and took her by the arm. Kaylee saw that Ellison did the same with Alana. Cory found some open space amid the hundreds of couples already swaying. They put their arms around each other and started to dance. Strangely, Kaylee knew the song. It was a standard her grandmother used to sing. Old Frank Sinatra. *Something's Gotta Give,* a song about what happens when the irresistible force of one person meets the immovable object of another person. When that happened, something had to give. It reminded Kaylee of herself and Zoey. Then, all thoughts of Zoey vanished as she gave herself over to the feeling of being in Cory's arms.

When the song was nearly over, she closed her eyes. That was when Cory kissed her for the very first time. Slow and steady. Intense. Soulful.

She opened her eyes and looked into his when the kiss was over.

When they finally separated, Kaylee noticed Alana. She was dancing with Ellison but staring at her. The hungry and jealous look in Alana's eyes made Kaylee wonder if maybe her boss was less over Cory than she claimed to be. That would not be good. Then Alana took Ellison by the arm and moved him to a part of the dance floor where they couldn't be seen.

"Did that just happen?" she asked Cory quietly. "You kissing me?"

"It did. Was it good or bad?"

"Good."

"Good," he murmured.

He kissed her again. It was very, very good.

WEDDING BELL BLUES

ALANA

BOOK 2

JEFF
GOTTESFELD

SADDLEBACK
EDUCATIONAL PUBLISHING

STRIPPED

Stripped
Wedding Bell Blues
Independence Day
Showdown on the Strip

SADDLEBACK
EDUCATIONAL PUBLISHING
www.sdlback.com

Copyright ©2014 by Saddleback Educational Publishing
All rights reserved. No part of this book may be reproduced in any form or by any means, electronic or mechanical, including photocopying, recording, scanning, or by any information storage and retrieval system, without the written permission of the publisher. SADDLEBACK EDUCATIONAL PUBLISHING and any associated logos are trademarks and/or registered trademarks of Saddleback Educational Publishing.

ISBN-13: 978-1-62250-769-6
ISBN-10: 1-62250-769-X
eBook: 978-1-61247-980-4

Printed in Guangzhou, China
NOR/0914/CA21401458

18 17 16 15 14   2 3 4 5 6

For Emma, Impressive #1.

MEET THE CHARACTERS

ALANA: Heiress Alana Skye, daughter of famous billionaire hotelier Steve Skye, is drop-dead gorgeous. But her life has been less than happy. And she has a difficult time living up to her father's demand for perfection.

CHALICE: Rich girl Chalice Walker is one of Alana's besties. Her ditzy, fun-loving nature masks an old soul. College is not for her because she's an artist at heart.

CORY: In the glitzy world of Vegas, Cory Philanopoulos was Alana's rock. Then he went to Stanford and everything changed. Back for the summer, rekindling a romance with Alana is not on his radar.

ELLISON: Why is Ellison Edwards working as a personal trainer in the luxurious LV Skye Hotel when he can afford any Ivy League school? And he has the brains to get accepted.

KAYLEE: No stranger to poverty and hardship, Kaylee Ryan literally falls into her dream job at the LV Skye. As Alana Skye's personal assistant, no less. Will poor girl Kaylee get along with Alana's rich besties?

REAVIS: From Texas like Kaylee, Reavis Smith is determined to make it big in Sin City. He's a street magician with a secret identity. And he's making a name for himself all over town.

ROXANNE: Supermodel Roxanne Hunter-Gibson is beauty and brains combined. She's managed to make a killing with an entrepreneurial start-up. Now she's Steve Skye's latest hot squeeze.

STEVE: Self-made man, cunning, rude (and some would say a lot worse) are some of the words used to describe hotel billionaire Steve Skye. And his crowning achievement is the luxurious LV Skye Hotel and Casino on the Las Vegas Strip.

ZOEY: Zoey Gold-Blum is the hottest rich girl in town. She knows it. And she uses it to her advantage. Deferring college for a year, she is out to keep her besties Chalice and Alana all to herself.

CHAPTER ONE

Alana Skye woke up thinking that it was a great day to be young, hot, and Sick Rich. One of the advantages of being rich was breakfast in bed whenever she wanted. It was always delivered by the butler, Mr. Clermont, and her order was always the same—a little pick-me-up before she got the day moving. Two cups of the LV Skye Hotel's house brand Indonesian coffee in a French press, one lightly buttered croissant, and a glass of filtered water drawn from the hotel's own well.

For anyone else, croissants in bed would be a risky choice because of the crumb factor. In Alana's case, the penthouse housekeeping crew changed her sheets daily whether she slept in them or not. So croissants were no problem. Alana could have scattered a ton of crumbs on

her bed and floor, and within hours they would be vacuumed and disposed of without so much as her making a phone call.

Alana had an easy life. But as her best friend, Zoey Gold-Blum, who also had an easy life, always said, "Alana? There's nothing to apologize for. It's an easy life, yeah. But someone's got to live it."

"Thank you, Mr. Clermont," Alana said when the butler had placed her tray on the side table. She was still in bed, with the 2,000-thread-count Egyptian cotton sheets pulled up to her chin.

"Very good, Miss Alana," Mr. Clermont told her. "Your friends Miss Zoey and Miss Chalice are awaiting you in the dining room. When you're ready."

"I'll be out in fifteen minutes," Alana said to the butler.

Zoey and Chalice had texted the night before to see if the three of them could meet up for coffee. They had something they wanted to talk over with her. It had been hard for Alana to find any time since she was so crazy busy these days with the LV Skye Hotel Teen Tower project. Once upon a time, the three girls pretty much owned the town and never came home before midnight. These days, with Teen Tower up and running, and Alana in charge again, Alana kept very different hours. For the last two weeks, she hadn't been to bed later than eleven.

WEDDING BELL BLUES

"Very well, Miss Alana," Mr. Clermont acknowledged. "Is there anything else?"

Alana shook her head. "No, Mr. Clermont. Thank you."

"Of course, Miss Alana."

He nodded gravely and left the room, tall and thin in his formal dark suit and tie. Alana had only ever seen him in a suit and tie, except when he came to work in a tuxedo. She couldn't imagine what Mr. Clermont looked like, say, in surfer jams and a UNLV Runnin' Rebels muscle shirt. The thought made her giggle. She'd pay to see that.

She poured and drank a little coffee, then got out of bed and stretched, cat-like. Her dark hair cascaded past her shoulders. There was a 270 degree mirror in her private bedroom suite, and she stepped into it and onto the scale. She smiled at herself—brown eyes flashing, full lips parting, but then frowned at the digits on the scale. She'd been working so hard at Teen Tower that she'd been eating on the fly, and she was six pounds over where she wanted to be. Ugh. She had work to do. But the unlimited Teen Tower dining room food was just so good.

"Coffee for breakfast," she mentally told herself. "Then the *Stripped* blog. Then Zoey and Chalice. And then Kaylee and work. I want my dad to see me working hard today."

9

One of the few things that made Alana's life less than perfection was her father. She was the only daughter of the great Steve Skye, for whom the LV Skye Hotel was named. The LV Skye was the flagship of the Skye empire of hotels and real estate. It was his baby, his pride and joy. It was the casino-hotel against which all other Las Vegas casino-hotels on Las Vegas Boulevard, otherwise known as the Strip, were judged.

The LV Skye was the biggest. It was the priciest. It had the best facilities. It had the most famous clientele. It had the fanciest casino, restaurants, indoor mall, convention center, spa, art gallery, and nightclubs in the city. Whenever there was an MMA title fight to be held in Vegas, it happened in an arena erected in the LV Skye parking lot. When rock and hip-hop artists came to Vegas, they stayed at the LV Skye, no matter where they were performing. It rose like a gold modernist sculpture above the Strip. Its fifty-five stories gleamed in the desert sun, with three thousand guest rooms that were always full.

The LV Skye was, quite simply, the greatest. It was also a money machine. Steve Skye made money from the rooms, the restaurants, the casino, the spa, the parking, the shops, and even the resort fees that guests paid for Internet use and the "free" bottles of water and box of Belgian chocolates in their rooms. It was a multi-billion

WEDDING BELL BLUES

dollar a year enterprise, run with an iron fist by Alana's father, who was grooming his daughter to take over when it was time for him to retire.

Steve was widely known as a bully. Charming to strangers, curt to those who worked for him, and driven beyond measure, he never failed to turn any conversation with Alana into a teachable moment about the hotel business. The difficulty for Alana was that until very recently she demonstrated no particular aptitude for the her father's business. She was a nice girl, bright enough, more than cute enough. She was also a good friend. But there were no signs that she'd inherited her father's business smarts, despite Steve's constant teaching, exhorting, encouraging, and shaming.

Then Steve Skye put Alana in charge of Teen Tower, his new teen-themed entertainment space at the hotel. Teen Tower operated on the same all-inclusive fee basis as many Caribbean and Mexican resorts, but the clientele was limited to kids between the ages of thirteen and eighteen. They—meaning, their parents, grandparents, or some other adult—dropped three figures a day so that the kids could eat, drink non-alcoholic beverages, play in a no-money casino, hang by the pool, and enjoy the game room and top-notch entertainment. Basically they had a place to go so they wouldn't make their parents' vacations miserable.

Alana had floundered at Teen Tower until she met Kaylee Ryan, a girl her age who had no education to speak of but a fantastic knack for making Teen Tower a cool place to be. Alana had made Kaylee her assistant, and Teen Tower had opened with an enormous splash. After just two weeks, Teen Tower was generating almost half a million dollars for the hotel every day. The profit margin was enormous. For the first time in her life, it seemed Steve Skye was totally happy with his daughter.

Alana slipped into a silk bra and panties, then went back to bed to do the first thing that anyone who was in the Vegas casino-hotel business did when they awakened: check the *Stripped* blog. *Stripped* was the Las Vegas newswire, gossip wire, entertainment wire, scandal wire, and business wire all rolled into one. Zoey's two mothers wrote it, and they had access to great information. When something big was happening in Vegas, they always heard about it first. Good, bad, scandalous, whatever.

She had a *Stripped* app on her iPhone. One touch and the blog came up. She scanned the stories, looking to see if there was anything relevant to Teen Tower or about the new street magician, Phantom. His feats of magic and illusion were dazzling the town. His real name was Reavis Smith. Kaylee knew him personally and had finally revealed his identity to Alana. She had even snuck him into Teen Tower to perform

WEDDING BELL BLUES

at the grand opening—which had restored Alana's dad's faith in her abilities, *and* gotten Kaylee's job back.

Kaylee and Alana wanted Phantom to perform at Teen Tower permanently. So far, though, he was content to do street magic and buff up his daredevil reputation.

Today's *Stripped* seemed normal. There was a clever and nasty review of a new Asian fusion restaurant near Caesar's Palace that the moms compared to Panda Express. Kiss of death. The place would have to close.

Then Alana saw something that made her sit up in her custom-made four-poster bed and take notice.

> Our sources tell us that Steve Skye's been spotted at Harry Winston Jewelers in Los Angeles, as well as at a certain diamond dealer on New York City's Forty-Seventh Street. Not to go out on a limb and make a prediction, but *Stripped* isn't *not* making a prediction either. Since his divorce from troubled model Carli Warshaw, we've counted eleven girlfriends for the town's hottest bachelor. Who knows? Maybe Roxanne is going to be the last one.
>
> Good luck, Roxanne. You'll need it.

Whoa, extra whoa, and maybe extra woe. Alana

frowned. Since the time he'd divorced her mother, Steve had indeed hooked up with eleven serious girlfriends. These relationships always followed the same course. Hot meeting, hot passion, hot split.

The latest girlfriend, Roxanne Hunter-Gibson, was as smart, as beautiful, and as young as all Steve's other girl-friends had been. In today's *Stripped*, Zoey's moms were intimating that this was a more serious relationship. That could be, but Alana decided they were guessing beyond the facts. Vegas was nothing if not all about odds. And Alana knew the odds that her playboy father was in a jewelry store to do anything but buy Roxanne a regular gift were slim to none. It made a good story, though. It would get the town talking.

There was a knock at her door.

"Hold a sec," she called, figuring it was Mr. Clermont.

"What's this 'hold a sec' bull? You've grown something you don't want us to see?"

Alana smiled. Zoey. She and Chalice must have gotten tired of waiting for her. "Come on in, you guys. I thought you were Mr. Clermont."

The door opened; Zoey and Chalice piled into her room. Zoey was tall and thin, with short hair and a size 0 body that the camera loved. She wore a short black dress and sandals.

WEDDING BELL BLUES

Chalice was smaller and curvier, with red ringlets. Her body was packed into a retro green-and-white polka dot dress. Alana had known both girls since her arrival in Las Vegas. Zoey was whip-smart, caustic, fierce, and forward. Chalice was sweet and fun-loving, and a genius with hair and cosmetics, but not the brightest bulb lighting the makeup mirror.

There were hugs all around. Her friends flopped down on Alana's bed. Alana spilled a little coffee on the white comforter in the process but didn't fret. That would be changed by the daily help too.

"Did you see *Stripped*?" Zoey asked bluntly.

"You mean the thing about my dad and Roxanne?" Alana asked.

Chalice clasped her hands together. "Isn't it romantic? Picking out a diamond."

Zoey made a face. "Please. First of all, she's like ten years older than we are. Second of all, he's not marrying her. He'd have to sleep with only her for the rest of his life."

"I still think it's romantic," Chalice opined. "I wish someone would buy me a diamond."

"Buy one for yourself and say it came from your lover in Paris," Zoey suggested.

"I don't have a lover in ... Oh! I get it. Well. Maybe

I will get myself a lover in Paris. I wonder how long that would take me."

Alana smiled. Chalice was always willing to laugh at herself. It was a good quality.

"So," she said to her friends. "There was something you wanted to talk to me about. Bring it."

Zoey and Chalice exchanged a serious glance that made Alana nervous.

"What?" Alana asked.

"We wanted to talk to you about—"

Before Zoey could go further, there was another knock on the door.

"Yes?" Alana called.

"Miss Alana, are you decent?" Mr. Clermont asked through the closed door. "Your father is on his way to see you."

"Tell him thirty seconds!" Alana looked back to Zoey and Chalice. "Hold that thought."

She got up and scrambled for her white terrycloth robe with the hotel monogram. She put it on just in time too. Her father knocked once and then opened the door. He was dressed in tennis clothes; he always hit for forty-five minutes on the hotel courts with the in-house pro before going to his office. He had a strong build and thick, dark hair. For a guy in his forties, he looked good.

WEDDING BELL BLUES

"Hey," he said gruffly, expressing no surprise that Zoey and Chalice were on the bed with Alana.

"Hi, Daddy. Is everything okay?"

Steve Skye shook his head and glared at Zoey. "No. Everything is not okay, thanks to Zoey's mothers. This is not the way that I intended for word to get out."

Alana startled. What had he just said? *This is not the way I intended for word to get out.*

Oh no! It was true. Steve and Roxanne were actually getting married. It was just a matter of when. She, Alana Skye, was going to get a stepmother. Like it or not.

CHAPTER TWO

Five minutes later, Chalice and Zoey were gone—asked to depart by Steve. Steve and Alana moved to the white-on-white penthouse living room, with its glass wall looking out at the Strip from the fifty-fifth floor of the hotel. Roxanne joined them. Steve was still in his tennis clothes. Alana wore nothing more than the white terrycloth robe and some floppy white slippers.

Roxanne was fresh, sharp, and perfectly made up. She had on the kind of expertly tailored outfit that Meryl Streep had worn in *The Devil Wears Prada*. Except Roxanne was two-fifths of Streep's age and wore the suit like the model she used to be. She was tall, thin, with thick curly hair and a regally long neck. Objectively, she was a beautiful

18

woman. Subjectively, she was the She-Devil Stepmother-To-Be From Another Planet.

Mr. Clermont brought in coffee. Alana sipped hers, knowing that she might need maximum caffeine fueling for this get-together, as well as for the day ahead. As she tried to fortify herself, she listened to her father's conversation. He was yammering on his cell phone with Zoey's mothers. From what she could hear, they were trying to get him to give them an exclusive interview about the upcoming nuptials, while Steve was doing his best to control his temper. Alana was aghast that this was how she was learning the details of the wedding. Not that she would share those feelings. She knew her dad would probably turn it into a teachable moment.

"So, again, Stacy and Sunshine. Here's what I can tell you." Alana knew her father's exasperated but controlled voice, and he was using it. "The wedding is going to be a week from Saturday here at the hotel. We'll probably do it in one of the ballrooms, though the ceremony may be upstairs in the nightclub. At least that's what we're thinking about. We're bringing in a wedding planner, so all that may change. Thanks to you, we've had to step up our planning. We don't know what the guest list will look like. ... No, I don't know who's officiating. ... Yes, it's short notice. ...

JEFF GOTTESFELD

Yes, we expect everyone we invite will come. We'll surely help with transportation. … Yes, you can expect an invitation. … Yes, I'll keep you informed. Now, can I click off so I can plan a wedding? ... Thank you."

Her father clicked off.

"Sorry about that," he muttered to Roxanne, as if Alana wasn't even there.

"It's fine, honey," Roxanne said. "You know those bloggers. They're like vultures."

"Except when you need them," Alana piped up brightly. "Then they're your best friends."

A look of anger crossed Steve's face, then he softened. "Listen, sweetie," he said to Alana. He picked up a small remote control on the end table next to his chair and pushed a button. The windows darkened to better block out the blazing desert morning sun. "This isn't the way that we intended to tell you. I know it must be a shock."

Alana's eyes widened. "Shock? No. Touching a live wire, that's a shock. This is open-heart surgery without anesthesia."

Steve actually smiled. "Nice simile. Glad to see that private school education is paying off."

Alana had one big question. It seemed sort of trivial and maybe even foolish, but it had been bothering her since Steve confirmed the wedding in her bedroom.

WEDDING BELL BLUES

"Do I have to be in the wedding?"

"Yes," Steve said immediately.

"No," Roxanne said at the exact same time.

Alana saw the two of them look at each other. Clearly, like so many other details, this hadn't been something they had discussed. To her surprise, Roxanne spoke up to explain before her father did. "What your dad means, Alana, is that he would like you to be in the wedding. So would I. That said, you're eighteen now. I seem to recall a birthday party just a few weeks ago, no?"

Alana nodded. That birthday party had been where she'd met Kaylee, which was the moment her life had begun to change for the better.

"Well, since you're eighteen, that means you're going to make your own decisions, and it's up to your dad and me to respect them. If there's a place for you in the wedding, we'll offer it to you. If you choose not to accept it, that's your decision, and we'll respect it. Isn't that right, Steve?"

Alana and Roxanne's eyes swung to Steve. "I would say that's right, Roxanne. But you'll help with the planning, right, Alana? I know you have a great sense of how to make an event beautiful."

Alana had all kinds of nasty retorts that she could make, most of them having to do with Roxanne's gorgeous chiseled face, legs that went on forever, and body that wouldn't

21

quit. She wondered if those gorgeous things weren't the reason that Steve was marrying her. Then again, he didn't have to marry anyone to ensure a constant stream of women who'd be happy to flow through his bedroom for one night or several. He was consistently on the list of the world's most eligible bachelors, both for his athletic good looks and the number of digits in his various bank accounts.

"I'm just glad you're happy," Alana said stiffly.

Steve looked ready to jump down her throat. After a knowing glance from Roxanne that Alana saw full well, he backed off. "Here's the thing, sweetie. It hasn't been easy for us since your mom got sick—"

"That's putting it lightly," Alana interjected sadly.

"I know. But I'm hoping that … well, I'm hoping that, over time, we can build a new family. Right here, right now."

Alana closed her eyes and thought back to when she was twelve. It wasn't all that long ago. Just six years. She, her dad, and her mom had lived in New York City then. Her father was running his hotel business out of his Manhattan office. The LV Skye was in the process of being built. It wouldn't open for another eighteen months. Though her mom, Carli, was a busy model who traveled a lot, and her dad was often away on business too, her dad's parents were always around. They loved their granddaughter. It wasn't

a conventional way to grow up, no. But it worked. Alana felt taken care of. The perks, like ski trips to the Alps, a limo and driver, and a Park Avenue apartment, were pretty great too.

Then just before Alana turned thirteen, it all fell apart. Her mother went nuts. She'd have fits of rage, followed by black depressions, followed by bursts of activity. She refused to go to a shrink, no matter how much Steve and his parents urged. Finally, she had a celebrated mental collapse on the runway right in the middle of the most important show of New York Fashion Week. The cameras were rolling, so Carli's screaming, cursing breakdown, as well as the Oscar de la Renta gown she tore to shreds with her bare hands, was captured for the whole world to see. There were whole websites devoted to the Carli Warshaw Meltdown, as it came to be known. The one on YouTube had more than ten million hits. It took four paramedics to get Carli onto a stretcher and then to the psych ward at New York-Presbyterian Hospital.

Carli spent time at that hospital, various rehabs, and then finally settled into a long-term care facility in Georgia. Her career was over. Her life as a mother was over. After three years, Steve divorced her. It hurt Alana terribly. But in a way, Alana understood. Despite the best doctors in the world and every manner of medication, there was

apparently no prospect that Carli would get better. Steve wanted to get on with his life; he had a new hotel to run in Las Vegas. Steve made sure that Carli had a huge trust fund for her care. She did not contest the divorce. Not that she had the mental capacity to do so.

Every so often, Alana would call the Georgia hospital, just to confirm that nothing had changed. Most of the time, her mother wouldn't even come to the phone. When she did, she was usually zombied out or wired to the point of incoherence, though on occasion Carli would have a few minutes of lucidity. This gave Alana hope that was inevitably dashed with the next call. Whatever was misfiring in her mother's brain, science hadn't yet progressed to where it could regulate those impulses. The result for Alana was a mother who could not mother.

Even so. The idea of her father remarrying? Of gaining a stepmother? Of being asked to build a new family? Well, that was sort of a joke.

"Okay. I'm up to speed. Can I get ready for work now, Dad?" Alana asked.

Again, Steve and Roxanne shared a significant look. Then Steve stood.

"Soon. Right now, I want you two to get better acquainted. After all, you're going to be family," Steve told her. "Roxanne, I'll see you in my office later."

WEDDING BELL BLUES

"Sure thing, Steve," Roxanne said casually as Alana's dad departed.

It was just the two of them now in the living room.

"Hi," Roxanne said.

"Hi."

"This has to be a surprise."

"Not really."

Roxanne raised her eyebrows. "No?"

"Nope. I read *Stripped* when I woke up," Alana deadpanned.

Roxanne laughed. "Always go with a reliable source, I say. Anyway, your dad has put the wedding in my hands. Everything. Location, food, decorations, music, invitations, etcetera, etcetera. Between you and me, I think it's as much a test of what I can do on short notice as it is anything else."

"My advice is, don't mess it up," Alana said drily.

"I don't intend to," Roxanne said. She finished the last of her coffee, and then put her cup back in its saucer. "I'd like for you to help me. If you can help me, I can help you."

"How?" Alana asked.

"Well, I can think of all kinds of things for you to do."

Alana folded her arms and pulled down the bathrobe a little. "No. I know how I can help you. What I was asking was how you can help me."

25

"I see." Roxanne uncrossed her legs. "Well, I have your dad's ear. And that's a good thing. But the fact is, I might be good for something else too." She leaned toward Alana and spoke sincerely. "I know the story of your mother. It has to be hard without her. Without any woman in your life you can talk to."

Ah. Alana got it. Roxanne was proposing to be her special confidante. The chances of that happening were between zero and zero. Alana didn't want to be rude, though. Roxanne deserved at least a few points for trying.

She stood, just like her dad had. "I'll see you later, Roxanne. Be good to me, and I'll be good to you. Good luck with my dad. Like *Stripped* said this morning, I think you're going to need it."

CHAPTER THREE

Alana was still reeling as she took the private elevator down from the penthouse, walked through the main lobby of the LV Skye, and then followed the labyrinth of corridors and hallways over to Teen Tower. Her father was getting married. The wedding would happen in less than two weeks. She was being asked to get buddy-buddy with Daddy's bride-to-be. It was like something out of the soap operas her mother used to love to watch when she wasn't out on the road. However, this was real. Alana was completely unprepared.

There was a little office Alana and Kaylee had set up on the second floor of Teen Tower. It had a couple of desks, some monitors, security equipment, a bunch of phones, and a few chairs. From the inside, she and Kaylee

JEFF GOTTESFELD

could look down on the Teen Tower pool deck through one-way glass. Kaylee was already there when she pushed open the door. Kaylee had her long blonde hair in a messy ponytail. No makeup covered her perky nose. Kaylee was one of those girls who looked pretty, but when she dressed up, watch out. She could be stunning. Alana had seen that firsthand on the night they'd first met.

"Hi, what are you up to?"

Kaylee resettled the phone handset on the receiver. "Just making sure things are together for the concert this afternoon."

Every afternoon, Teen Tower featured a band, singer, or hip-hop artist on the stage by the pool deck. The concert was broadcast live on MTV. It was a favorite feature of the Teen Tower day.

"Are they?"

"Totally."

Alana grinned despite her anguish. "Why am I not surprised? You're Miss Efficiency."

"I try to be."

Alana steadied herself. Saying it would make it real. "What are you doing a week from tomorrow?"

Kaylee shrugged. "Beats me. I'll be here, I guess. Why?"

28

"No, you won't. I mean, you'll be here at the hotel, but you won't be at Teen Tower. You're going to a wedding. I'm going to a wedding. We're all going to a wedding."

"Really? Whose?"

"You read *Stripped* this morning?"

"Sure," Kaylee said.

"It's true," Alana confirmed. "My dad. And Roxanne. And a couple thousand of their closest friends."

"What?! They can't be getting married. They—they practically just met!"

Alana was happy to hear Kaylee's surprise. It confirmed to her that she wasn't crazy to be this flipped out—that the idea of Steve Skye marrying Roxanne Hunter-Gibson was something that would play great in the tabloids, but not in the reality of her own life.

Alana folded her arms and bit her lower lip. "Well, they're getting married anyway. They told me this morning. And you and I are helping out with the wedding. In our copious free time. Get prepared for some long days and longer nights."

Alana watched as Kaylee stood and moved to the window. She wondered what her new assistant thought of all this. Vegas was known for quick weddings, that was for sure. Nevada had the loosest marriage requirements in

the country. There were rent-by-the-hour wedding chapels everywhere. A person could even find a wedding officiant who looked like Elvis Presley.

"What do you think?" Kaylee asked.

"About them getting married?"

"Is there another topic?"

"I guess not."

"So …?"

Alana leaned back in her chair and closed her eyes, then pressed her thumbs against her eyelids so her eyes actually hurt. She opened them again and looked at Kaylee. "Well, I can safely say that what I think doesn't matter. It was presented to me as a *fait accompli*. Meaning, a done deal."

"But how do you feel?"

That question again. From a girl who she didn't know all that well. Kaylee was smart. And she was talented. That was for sure. But they'd only known each other for a few weeks. It still felt weird talking about such personal stuff with her. It wasn't like Kaylee was Zoey, or even Chalice.

"I'm not exactly jumping up and down at the idea of a stepmother who is technically young enough to be my sister. Roxanne kinda proved herself to be a first class witch to me when we were starting up Teen Tower. You were here, you saw it. So forgive me if I'm not clamoring to be maid of honor. Not that they asked me specifically."

"Well, maybe it'll get canceled."

Alana shook her head. That Kaylee would say such a thing betrayed her naïveté. She had no experience with this kind of thing. And certainly she had no experience with how Steve Skye operated. "Oh, it'll happen. It's already in *Stripped*. It'll be too embarrassing for my dad to back out now. Lucky me. Look. It's between the two of them. I wish them all the luck in the world."

"I don't believe you," Kaylee said quietly.

"I'm not asking you to."

Alana took a deep breath. It wasn't fair to get down on Kaylee for her lack of experience or lack of familiarity with the ins and outs of Alana's own life. Kaylee was who she was. And wasn't who she wasn't. She decided to change the subject to something less close to home. "What's going on in your love life? I haven't asked in a while."

"Love life? I have a love life?" Kaylee asked with a sly grin. Then she quickly filled Alana in on the latest with Reavis—the magician who performed as Phantom—and with Ellison, the guy who ran the Teen Tower gym. It wasn't much. Reavis was busy working on magic tricks and performing occasionally, with Kaylee as his assistant. Ellison had shown some interest in Kaylee when Teen Tower had first opened, but Kaylee said that his interest had moved from romantic to friendly.

Alana voiced a sudden thought. Had Kaylee ever even had a boyfriend?

The answer was no.

"You know how I grew up," Kaylee explained. "And where I lived. It's not like Echo Park in Los Angeles is full of guys I was dying to date. Same thing with my grandmother's trailer park."

"Well, now you're here. There's no shortage of quality guys," Alana declared. "I like Cory. He's been my only serious boyfriend. If only he liked me back as much as I like him."

Cory Philanopoulos. That was the guy she wanted. They'd been boyfriend and girlfriend before Cory went away to college. Cory was a fine guy. Tall, rangy, sandy-haired, and a water polo player. They'd not talked at all while Cory was away at Stanford. Then, when he came home, he'd confessed to Alana that he'd had a major depressive episode that had nearly wrecked his entire freshman year. Not as bad as what her own mother had experienced, and not manic depression, but bad.

Alana liked him more for having shared that with her. She'd offered him a job at Teen Tower in the social media department. And he took it because he didn't want to spin his wheels all summer. The job was certainly not for the money, since Cory's father ran a mega-successful hedge

32

fund with assets in the hundreds of billions of dollars. Everyone was rooting for an Alana-and-Cory rerun. Alana, Zoey, Chalice, and Kaylee. All that had to happen was for Cory to be convinced too. They'd seen each other quite a bit since Cory came on board at Teen Tower. But, like Kaylee and Ellison, it felt more buddy-buddy than cuddly-cuddly.

"You guys are going out a lot," Kaylee said. "Right?"

"Yeah. But it's like … just friends. I don't want to be just friends with him."

"Don't rush it," Kaylee cautioned.

Okay. This was ironic coming from Kaylee, who had as much experience with guys as Alana had with doing her own laundry. That is, none.

"Why should I listen to you?" she asked. "You've never had a boyfriend!"

Kaylee's charming, tinkling laughter filled the little office. "Okay, you're right. But still. You know, I can maybe talk to him for you."

"You mean, like with a guy in the middle school cafeteria?" The idea sounded faintly ridiculous. "Where you say, 'Alana likes you, do you like her?' and then report back to me?"

"No!" Kaylee exclaimed. "More to, like, say nice things about you to him."

Alana thought it over. Well then. It was kind of middle school but also kind of smart. Unless Kaylee was an idiot—and Kaylee was not an idiot—her talking with Cory about Alana couldn't hurt. In fact, it might even help.

"Okay," Alana agreed. "But don't be too obvious." She stood and smoothed out the back of her T-shirt. "Anything else I need to know before we go down? Let's meet for lunch at one."

Kaylee did have one more thing. She shared with Alana that she'd received a call from her crazy meth-head aunt, Karen, with whom she'd rented an apartment in Los Angeles right before coming to Vegas. Karen had allegedly gone to San Francisco after she and Kaylee had been evicted. Apparently, Karen was threatening to come to Vegas.

Alana was grateful to have a problem that she knew how to handle. She'd call her father, they'd circulate Karen's photo among the security staff, and if the woman so much as showed her face at the LV Skye, she'd be escorted off the premises. No way would she let this drugged-out woman hurt Kaylee, Teen Tower, or anyone or anything else.

"Don't worry about a thing," she told Kaylee. "She's not going to bother you."

"Don't hurt her."

Alana shook her head "No one's hurting anyone. But if she shows up here, we've got your back. I'm glad you told me what's going on. Now, let's get to work. We've got a Teen Tower to run."

"And a wedding."

"Lucky us."

As they headed for the elevator to the main level, Alana checked her phone. There were three texts from Zoey and Chalice, reminding her that they'd wanted to talk, and suggesting that they meet in the main lobby of the hotel. Alana texted them and said she was on her way.

Ten minutes later, she was sitting across from them in one of the main lobby's many sitting areas. Her father had designed the lobby to be cool, expansive, and calm, unlike the frenetic lobby atmosphere at so many lesser Strip hotels. The corner that Zoey and Chalice had chosen had three white leather couches, two chairs, and a marble coffee table. A harpist was playing Georg Philipp Telemann about fifty feet away at just the perfect volume.

Her friends stood to embrace her. "How are you?" Zoey asked, taking her by the shoulders when the hugs were over. "No. Don't answer that. That's a stupid question. You're wrecked."

Alana nodded. "Yeah. Pretty much. How much do you know?"

"A lot," Chalice related.

"This whole thing sucks," Zoey moped. "Sit."

They sat as one on the same couch. Chalice to the left, Alana in the center, and Zoey to the right. Zoey slung an arm around Alana's shoulder. It felt great.

"Anyway, here's what you need to know. We're here for you through this whole thing. Me and Chalice," Zoey said. "Alone, together, however. Anytime, day or night. And if you feel like you've got to get out of that penthouse, you come to my place."

"Or my place," Chalice said helpfully.

"Whichever. You're our friend, you've been our friend for a long time, and we love you," Zoey declared. "Okay?"

Alana nodded.

That wasn't enough for Zoey. "I asked, 'okay?'"

"Okay," Alana declared.

"Okay!" Zoey and Chalice said at the same time, then laughed.

Alana liked Kaylee a lot. A lot, a lot, even. But she wasn't the same as Zoey and Chalice. History in relationships mattered, she realized. Nothing could replace it.

"What did you guys want to talk to me about?" Alana asked suddenly. They'd come to her that morning with something urgent; it had been lost in the tumult of the wedding announcement.

"Actually, it's kind of like this, right now," Chalice began.

Zoey nodded. "We were missing you. It's been a long time since we've really hung out. You're so busy at Teen Tower—"

Alana put up a hand. She'd had a sudden thought and couldn't believe she hadn't thought of it before.

"Hold on. I am such an idiot."

"What?" Chalice asked.

"You miss me. I miss you. And I'm running the coolest place to be in Vegas if you're a teen." Alana giggled. Her idea was so obvious.

She pointed at Chalice. "You."

Then she pointed at Zoey. "And you." And then she pointed at both of them. "You guys need to come work at Teen Tower, and I am not taking no for an answer."

CHAPTER FOUR

All things considered, it wasn't a bad night to gamble. The day had been pretty brutal, what with the wedding announcement and everything. What was good had been Alana's genius decision to ask Zoey and Chalice to join the Teen Tower staff. Looking back, Alana couldn't believe that she hadn't done that right from the beginning, even though her two besties hadn't exactly been clamoring to work for her. They had plenty of money. Their plan for the summer had been slumming, swimming, and flirting with hot guys. The summer could stretch into October for all they cared.

Like Alana, neither of her besties was going away to college in the fall. Alana had decided to wait a year to apply, while Zoey had deferred for a year at New York

University. Chalice wasn't planning to do college at all. She was hoping her father would set her up with her own salon and spa. But she needed some business experience under her belt before Daddy would put up the cash.

It was for that reason that Alana assigned Chalice to work in Teen Tower's new makeover pavilion, where she'd take photographs of guests getting their hair and makeup done. Then she'd post them to the Teen Tower Tumblr. As for Zoey, she spent her first day on the job as a "motivator" at the pool, helping to rev up the party and get kids involved in games and contests.

Come nightfall, Alana was happy to go out. Kaylee had suggested that maybe they could visit an underground, not-very-legal casino club she'd heard of in North Las Vegas. She'd even invite Cory to come along. Alana loved the idea. This could be the time when Cory would do the right thing, the smart thing, and the obvious thing: show her some sign that he was ready to be her boyfriend again.

Just in case, though, she covered her bets. Since Kaylee said she wasn't interested in Ellison in "that way," Alana stopped by the Teen Tower gym where he worked and mentioned to Ellison that she'd be going to the underground casino and asked if maybe he would want to drop by. He was eye candy, for sure. The Teen Tower gym was

attracting more girl guests than guy guests. Alana figured it was because of the finest candy bar of all: Ellison Edwards. He was very tall, very dark, very handsome, and very, very buff.

The strangest thing of all was that Ellison already knew about Cory.

"What's up with you and Cory?" Ellison had asked as they'd stood together by the check-in desk at the gym. Alana had been doing a routine pass through the gym when she struck up the conversation with Ellison.

"What about him?" Alana had asked coyly.

"Well … I haven't been in Vegas all that long, but I know that you two used to go together. I hear you wouldn't mind if that happened again."

Alana had nodded coolly. "That's true." She felt no reason to hide the truth here. "I wouldn't mind. But that doesn't mean he's going to feel the same way I do. And if he doesn't … well, it's going to be a long summer. I'd hate to spend it alone. You know?"

A slow smile had spread over Ellison's friendly face. "Ah. You're talking about an arrangement. Very Henry James. But you're no Isabel Archer, and I'm no Gilbert Osmond."

Alana was no great shakes as a student, but she had read *The Portrait of a Lady* and got the reference.

"And you're no Pansy either," she quipped, dropping the name of Gilbert's daughter in the famous classic novel.

Ellison had laughed at that—a long, rolling, masculine laugh that sort of made Alana's knees weak. How could a guy be this smart, this athletic, and this masculine at the same time? The only other person she could think of who was like that was Cory Philanopoulos. If Cory wasn't willing to hang with her, it was good to hear that Ellison might be. That was when Alana had mentioned the outing to the casino. Ellison was into it. He said he'd meet her there.

The underground casino had no official name. It was in the middle of the city's warehouse district. Not really underground, it was located in a building that looked from the outside like any of the other warehouses. Inside, though, was a small gambling establishment where teens could actually go and play. Since it was set up as a private club with memberships, it was technically legal. Technically.

Alana saw Ellison inside soon after she and Kaylee had been dropped off by their limo driver. After a happy reunion at the "coincidence" of them both being there, they sent Kaylee off to play blackjack, then wandered around the casino together. They found Cory at a roulette table with a stack of chips in front of him. Ellison said a quick

hello, and then he gallantly absented himself as Alana sat next to Cory and bought into the game.

As was her habit, she put a bunch of five dollar chips on a color—either red or black—and then one chip on a single number. If the little ball ended up in the right color slot, she'd be paid one-for-one for the chips on the color. If the ball ended up, somehow, on the number she'd chosen, she'd be paid at thirty-six to one. The house had the advantage in the game, though. There were two green numbers: zero and double zero. Those two numbers were the house edge right there. The payoff should be at thirty-eight to one, but it wasn't. That's why the casino business was so lucrative. The games were stacked in favor of the house.

Cory hugged her when she sat down, but as usual, it felt more friendly than romantic. "You shouldn't play roulette, you know," he told her as she put five chips on red and a single chip on the number nineteen. "It's a sucker's game."

"You sound like my father," Alana said.

"Who I hear is about to be a married man," Cory quipped. He looked great in khaki slacks and a maroon cashmere sweater.

They were silent for a moment as the roulette attendant—known as the croupier—signaled no more bets, and then rolled the ball into the spinning wheel. As usual, the

WEDDING BELL BLUES

ball clattered around for a while before coming to rest on seventeen. A black number. She'd lost on the color and lost on her single play. Oh well. It was only money.

"True. And I am not about to be a maid of honor." Alana put more chips on red, while Cory spread out six or seven on single numbers around the table.

"Know anything more about the wedding?" Cory asked.

"Do you want to be my date?" Alana asked him.

Cory laughed as the croupier rolled the ball into the spinning wheel. It clattered around again, this time coming to rest on the number three.

"Yes!" Cory exclaimed, punching the air. He had a single chip on three, which meant he was paid off at thirty-six to one. The croupier cleared the board of all the losing chips, and then pushed a big stack in Cory's direction. Alana doubled her money too, and let it ride. If red hit again, she'd be off to a good start on the night.

"So, what do you think? Want to be my date?" Alana asked. This was more forward than she'd ever intended to be, but what the hell. It was better to know where she really stood instead of following Cory around like a puppy, hoping that master would toss her a Milk-Bone. Besides. She had backup now in Ellison. It was a lot easier to operate with backup.

43

Cory laughed easily. "Hey. I don't even know if I'm invited. Your dad and Roxanne might run away to Reno and elope."

Alana didn't laugh. She knew that he was turning her down in the nicest possible way.

"Come on," Cory said. "That was funny."

"You didn't answer my question," Alana said pointedly.

"Actually, I did." Cory's voice was kind. "Let's see what the invitations say. And then let's talk." His voice got quieter. "You have to remember what I told you when we had dinner together, Alana. I'm moving slowly these days. I might look fine from the outside, but I'm not so fine on the inside. And I'm trying to find a way forward without making myself worse than 'not so fine,' you know?"

Alana nodded. She'd had breakfast with Cory just before Teen Tower had opened. He'd shared the details of his episode at Stanford. He'd required serious psychological help and a lot of prescription drugs. She understood when he said that he wanted to move slowly.

"You do look normal on the outside," she told him as she put a few chips on different numbers, straddling a couple of them on the line. If the ball landed on either of the numbers she straddled, she'd be paid at eighteen to one. Not bad odds.

For his part, he put a big stack of chips on black.

44

WEDDING BELL BLUES

"Thanks. It's funny. When I was with the docs, they tried to make my life as simple as they could. Eat healthy. Sleep lots. Move my body. They weren't even thinking about my schoolwork. That would come later." He turned to her. "Everything had to come later," he said. Then he put a hand on top of hers. "Everything."

"I understand," she replied even though she was hurting inside. "It doesn't mean I'm going to stop wanting you."

"We feel how we feel," Cory said flatly.

The croupier spun the wheel—they both watched as the ball landed on double zero. Losers all around. There was a collective groan from the people at the table. Alana remembered that Steve always called that groan "the groan of profit."

"We sure do." Alana stood. "You know what? I'm going to stretch my legs."

"That's a good idea." He stood too. "So, I'll catch up with you later."

"Hey, I hope so," Alana said bravely.

He smiled. "You can count on it."

She headed off into the casino and looked around. Ah! There was Ellison, playing craps. There was a spot next to him at the table, and she went right for it. She smiled as she realized that life was very much a crap shoot, and that she'd just crapped out with Cory.

45

CHAPTER FIVE

Okay." Ellison pointed to the low bench. "Next up for you, chest presses with dumbbells. But instead of pushing them two at a time, I want you to punch them. One hand, then the other." He made fists with his hands and punched the air with each hand one at a time. "One, two, three, four. Go till you can't go anymore. Got it?"

"Got it." Alana took her place on the bench. It was seven thirty in the morning. She and Ellison had the gorgeous Teen Tower gym to themselves. Not even the cleaning guys were on duty at this hour.

It was the day after the excursion to the casino in the warehouse. All things considered, Alana decided that the night hadn't gone too badly. It had been disappointing, for

sure, that Cory had rejected her when she'd suggested that he be her date for the wedding. She'd seen him playing blackjack near Kaylee for most of the evening. Kaylee had reported that she'd said all kinds of nice things about her to Cory. That was good. Maybe it would yield results at some point.

What was also good was that she had spent a lot of the evening with Ellison. She decided he was an incredibly cool guy. There was this brainy edge about him that was so unexpected from a guy so buffed up. It was like he was the smartest person in the room, and he knew it too. But he wasn't obnoxious about it the way that her dad was.

When Ellison had suggested that maybe she would want to start training in the morning to get into tiptop shape for the wedding, and that he would be happy to train her, she'd jumped at it. First, she still had six pounds to lose. Second, it meant that if she chose to wear something sleeveless, she'd look awesome. Third, the idea of private one-on-one training with Ellison was enough to get any girl's heart pounding. Best of all was that the two of them training gave them plausible deniability in the unlikely event that anyone was to walk in on them.

Her father frowned on romantic relationships between

management and low-level staff at the LV Skye. She was definitely management, and Ellison was definitely low-level staff.

Ellison handed her a couple of five-pound dumbbells. "Slow and steady, but don't stop. On my signal. Go."

At Ellison's okay, Alana did her dumbbell presses. For the first five pairs of pushes, it was reasonably easy. But she was not used to working out, and it got tough in a hurry. By the seventh up-down, she could only get part way through the "up" before she felt ready to collapse.

"That's it!" she declared as her arms turned to rubber, and she let the dumbbells drop to the ground.

"Tomorrow you'll hurt. Soon, you won't," Ellison told her. "And you'll feel the difference by the wedding. I guarantee it."

As the workout went on, Alana realized that she'd had no idea what she was in for. Ellison worked her hard, doing many repetitions with light weights. They did chest, biceps, and abs—tomorrow would be back, triceps, and abdominals again. Then he put her on one of the computerized bikes and climbed onto one next to her. Together they ran intervals. She pedaled at top speed for ten seconds and rested for fifty; he did top speed for forty seconds and rested for twenty. After twelve intervals like this, she was dripping with perspiration.

WEDDING BELL BLUES

"That's it for the day," he called when she professed being on the verge of a coronary. "No need to cool down, no need for stretching, that's urban myth stuff. You think LeBron does a cool down when he comes off the court after a game? You think he runs ten low-speed laps around the court after the final buzzer? No way. He goes to the locker room and takes a shower. Which is what you need to do. After you rehydrate."

They climbed down off their bikes and moved to the fitness desk. Ellison went behind it, opened a small fridge, and extracted a couple bottles of the hotel's private-label water. He cracked them open and handed her one. She put down the towel she was using to mop her brow and drank half the bottle in one gulp.

"You just killed me," she accused good-naturedly.

"Wait until you wake up tomorrow morning," he warned. "You'll be hurting."

"Well, I'm sure you know what to do with sore muscles," Alana said a bit flirtatiously.

Ellison smiled. "I've got some skills."

"I'm sure you have," Alana agreed. She drained the rest of the water. "Maybe I'll get a chance to see them."

"Maybe you will." His voice turned a little serious. "For sure, if you keep this up with me, you're going to be happier with your body. In every possible way. And you're

49

going to be more aware of the body that the good Lord gave you. In every possible way."

She smiled. When she was with Ellison, Cory seemed pretty far away. "Well. That sounds good to me. In every possible way."

If it wasn't for a meeting an hour later about the wedding, she might have stayed to discuss the various possible ways. Instead, she went to the locker room to shower and change, happier than she'd been in a really long time.

There was something about arriving from a workout with Ellison that made the big wedding planning meeting a lot more bearable. That the meeting was in the penthouse made it more bearable still. That her dad had suggested that Zoey and Chalice might want to help with the wedding planning was a big plus too.

Best of all, when she got there, she found that her father had truly decided to leave the wedding planning in Roxanne's hands and had gone to his office instead of sitting in on the discussion. He was a notorious micromanager. Alana had no doubt he'd be tempted to micromanage this too.

Alana arrived at the same time as Zoey and Chalice. Each commented on her glowing skin and big smile.

50

WEDDING BELL BLUES

"What are you so happy about?" Zoey asked. "I would think this would be like going to an execution."

Alana shook her head. "I'm training. In the gym."

"With Billy Blanks? Didn't he used to stay here?" Chalice asked.

Alana laughed. "Nope. With Ellison. You know, the guy in the Teen Tower gym."

"Mr. Tall Dark and Handsome? With the muscles like pool balls?" Zoey asked pointedly. "How can you even focus on the workout?"

Alana thought for a moment about confiding that maybe her interest in Ellison was something more than just as a trainer, and then decided to let it go. Who knew what would happen with Cory. She didn't know how Zoey or Chalice would react. Maybe they'd think she was two-timing Cory. To her, the idea of two-timing someone who was showing no particular readiness to one-time with you was kind of a crazy concept, but that was just her.

"He's buff," Chalice said admiringly.

"He's a good trainer," Alana said diplomatically.

"Hey, Alana? We're in here." Alana could hear Roxanne calling from the penthouse living room.

Alana led her friends into the penthouse with a brief hello for Mr. Clermont. She found Roxanne with the wedding planner, Abra Floyd, who had been flown in from

51

Manhattan. Abra was in her forties. She had the longest black braid that Alana had ever seen. She wore an orange fitted top and black trousers. The whole effect reminded Alana of Halloween, but Abra had planned many celebrity weddings and was even said to have been involved in the marriages of various British royalty. Putting a wedding together in eight days would be nothing for her.

There was an LV Skye business meeting breakfast on the marble coffee table—juices, carafes of coffee, and pastries. During her workout, Ellison had talked to Alana about the importance of eating right if she wanted to drop those six pounds, and carbs were not on his list of approved eats. He wanted her to eat lots of protein and stay away from sugar. All she took was a half cup of coffee; she'd have a healthy breakfast in one of the hotel dining rooms when the meeting was over.

"So," Abra said when they were all seated. She had a significant New York accent. "We're here to do a wedding. I'm here to do it, and you are along for the ride." She turned to Roxanne. "Actually, we're here for you. Our job is to make this the most unforgettable day of your life."

It was weird. As Abra talked about Roxanne and Steve's wedding, for one fleeting instant Alana had a vision of her own marriage someday in the future. She

closed her eyes and pictured a church—not a big one, a little one, out in the country someplace. There were cars parked in front, and well-dressed people were heading inside, though she stood outside. They were speaking a language that Alana didn't understand at first. Then she got it. They were speaking French. She'd taken French in high school and had actually been okay at it. This fantasy wedding of hers was happening somewhere in the French countryside. It was a glorious day, sunny and cool, and the air smelled of fresh tree pollen and lavender.

But who was her husband? Who was she marrying? She felt if she could just stay in this daydream, she could wait until he came out of the church to spend a few quiet moments with—

"Alana? Are you with us?" Abra's voice cut into her consciousness.

Alana opened her eyes. Whoa. That was quite a flight of fancy. Not like her to do that. If only she could have seen who she was marrying. She felt like it would tell her something important—a sort of supernatural message about her life from the great beyond.

"Yes, I'm here," she said softly. "I was just thinking. Sorry."

"Okay," Abra said. "Let's plan a wedding. Roxanne, what do you have in mind?"

All eyes shifted to Alana's stepmother-to-be. Alana had never seen her flustered. But Roxanne was flustered now. In fact, Alana couldn't believe what happened next. As they all watched, wanting to look away but unable to do so because the sight was so compelling, Roxanne started to weep.

CHAPTER SIX

It was beyond awkward. Sitting with Zoey, Chalice, and the wedding planner she'd known for about five minutes, watching the bride-to-be crying. Alana saw Zoey smirk. She herself just felt embarrassed for Roxanne.

Abra smiled knowingly. "This is an awesome moment. You're not the first bride to cry in my presence, Roxanne. You won't be the last. Here, I've got tissues." She opened her Fendi bag and handed over a pack of tissues. Alana wondered how many packs she went through in a year.

"Thank you," Roxanne told her, dabbing at her eyes. "It's just that ... well, if you knew where I came from, you might be crying too."

"I've planned about five hundred weddings," Abra said. "You can't imagine the stories I've heard. Tell me yours."

Alana wondered what Roxanne meant by what she'd said. Just like she would for anyone, she had done a routine Google search of her dad's girlfriend—no, his fiancée. She'd learned that Roxanne had grown up back east, went to public school and then Brown University. She began modeling while she was in high school. After Brown, she went out on the high-fashion trail full time, nabbing the covers of various European magazines and doing runway work all around the world.

Somehow, she found a way to go to business school in the middle of all of that, started a successful vacation and luxury travel channel and website, and sold it three years later for a ton of bucks. One thing was for sure. Roxanne did not have to marry Steve for his money. Not that Steve's bank account didn't dwarf hers, but she had plenty of chip. If she didn't want to work another day in her life, she didn't have to. Alana respected her for that and expected that Steve did too. There would be a prenup, but the marriage wasn't happening because Roxanne was a gold digger.

Still. Did she want to marry someone who was old enough to be her father?

"My parents came to this country from Africa," Roxanne explained. "From Ghana. I was born there, actually. We came with nothing. Maybe one suitcase. I don't remember the flight. I was little, but I've seen the picture.

My mom and dad, they never went to school. That here I am, who I am, what I've done, and who I'm about to marry?" She shook her head in disbelief. "It just doesn't seem real. Sorry for the waterworks, guys."

Alana was touched. Apparently so was Abra. For about a split second.

"You can talk about that when you toast Steve at the reception," the wedding planner said. "Now, we've got a wedding to plan and about an hour to figure out what we want to do and how we want to do it. Roxanne, what do you have in mind?"

Roxanne rubbed her chin thoughtfully, her tears forgotten. "Well, I've always wanted an outdoor wedding—"

"Are you out of your mind?" Zoey interjected. "This is Las Vegas. It's June. You're going to set up chairs and make people sit in the sun? You better have about five hundred ambulances because everyone will get sunstroke. Even if you do the wedding at night, they're going to melt unless you want the wedding to be informal, and I don't think you want that."

Roxanne looked chagrined. "Yeah. I guess you're right. I hadn't thought of that."

"No matter what we decide, none of this is going to leak to your moms, right, Zoey?" Abra asked sharply.

"No. It won't," Alana spoke up.

Zoey shook her head. "If there's a leak, it won't be from me."

"Because if it gets into the blog that there's disagreement about what the wedding should be, Steve is going to look bad, and then it falls on me," Abra pronounced. "I don't like to look bad. No leaking."

"No one's leaking. Right, Chalice?" Alana looked over at her friend, who made the sign of zipping her lips and throwing away the key.

"No one's asking me, but here's what I would do if I were you, Roxanne. I'd get the governor to do the wedding," Zoey declared. "He's up for reelection. He'll appreciate the photo-op. Have the rehearsal dinner at Mondrian. That's for family. Do the ceremony at some public place. Maybe the governor's office or someplace like that. Then do the party here at the hotel in the Desert Ballroom. Have breakfast the next day for out-of-town guests at the Hash House. It's the most famous breakfast place in town. Rent out the whole restaurant. Whaddaya think?"

Alana grinned. Leave it to Zoey to come up with a great plan without even much thought. Like Kaylee, Zoey had a real practical side to her.

"Whatever she thinks," Abra said nodding at Roxanne. "I think it's wonderful. And best of all, it's achievable."

WEDDING BELL BLUES

"I like it. I like it a lot!" Roxanne beamed at Zoey.

"Thank you. I mean, there's still a lot of work that has to be done, but that at least gives you a structure," Zoey said.

"I want your friend Zoey working with me this week as much as you can spare her," Abra told Alana.

"Done," Alana said.

"So that's settled," Abra declared. "Roxanne, I want you to go with Alana to room forty-three fifteen. You're getting fitted for a wedding gown. I've got it all set up. Go on!" She looked at her cell. "By my count, you've got a hundred and ninety-two hours till the biggest moment of your life. Every hour is precious."

Just as Alana was about to stand, she had another flash of her own wedding. She was still in France, still in front of the little country church. This time, she was conscious of her wedding gown. It was white chiffon with ice-blue accents on the shoulders and bustline and a sweetheart neckline. The train was immense, also in white chiffon. Three children in white dresses carried the train so it wouldn't drag in the spring grass. As before, she was waiting for her fiancé to come out of the church to meet her. As before, the vision was over before she could see the face of her fiancé. She concentrated to see if his image would come into her head. Was it Cory?

JEFF GOTTESFELD

Concentrating told her nothing. Her mind went blank. It was crazy. Why was this happening? Something important was going on here, and she didn't know what it was.

Two hours later, Roxanne and Abra were on the phone with Vera Wang. Vera described what she had in mind. Roxanne was enthralled. Then Abra took over and made arrangements for Vera and her team to fly to Las Vegas for a final fitting. The dress would be ready in plenty of time for the ceremony. After the choice had been made, a team of tailors had taken more measurements than if they were custom-designing an astronaut's spacesuit.

Through the whole process, Roxanne was unfailingly polite and cooperative. She gave Alana no additional reason to hate on her.

When they were done, Alana should have returned to Teen Tower. A lot of the morning had been burned on wedding stuff. But there was something she wanted to do, and she wanted Zoey to be included. She texted Zoey to meet her. Together they went back up to the penthouse, said hello to Mr. Clermont, who stood like a sentry by the elevator entrance, and went to her room.

"I don't think I've ever showed you this before," Alana said. She moved to her walk-in closet, which was the size of a medium jetliner, and dug out a footstool.

60

WEDDING BELL BLUES

"What? Your thigh-high boots and handcuffs?"

"I don't have thigh-highs and handcuffs. That would be you."

"Not anymore," Zoey joked. "I've moved on to more chaste modes of self-expression."

Alana laughed. "And for me, it would mean I'd have someone to play with, which I don't."

"Keep working on Cory," Zoey advised.

"He's not easy."

"Nothing good ever is," Zoey pronounced. "What's the big secret?"

Alana climbed on the footstool and hunted around on the shelf above her blouses. What she was looking for was up there somewhere.

"Got it!" she said, taking out a thick leather-bound book.

"Family Bible?" Zoey asked when she saw the volume.

"Almost. Come with me."

She led Zoey back near her bed and motioned for her friend to sit with her on the thick Berber carpet. "I don't look at this very often," Alana admitted.

"What is it?"

Alana flipped the first page.

Zoey whistled when she saw what this book actually was—the photo album from the wedding of Steve Skye

and Carli Warshaw. The date of the wedding, twenty years before, was imprinted on the leather cover. The very first picture was their classic wedding pose. Steve in a black tux with a bow tie; Carli in a white dress with a sweetheart neckline and a demure veil. Carli was tucked in against Steve's shoulder. Like Roxanne, she was nearly as tall as he was.

"They're so young," Zoey murmured.

"Not much older than we are," Alana said. "He was twenty-five when they married. She was twenty-one."

Zoey seemed fascinated. "Show me more."

Alana turned the page. The wedding had been early in Steve's storied career. He'd been wealthy then, but not filthy rich. The ceremony and reception had been at the Plaza Hotel; he and Carli had arrived in a horse drawn carriage. There were pictures of everything. The arrival, the procession, the service, the party. Steve seemed so happy. So did Carli.

"Cute couple," Zoey pronounced when Alana had finished showing her the pages of the album.

"I miss my mom," Alana confessed.

"How long has it been since she lost it? Seven years? Six?"

"Six. But I still wonder what she would think about Dad getting married again. Or how I'm supposed to feel."

Alana felt a lump rise in her throat. "I already have one mother. I don't need another one."

Zoey cleared her throat. "Well, the two mothers thing, that's up to you. I can say it kinda worked out for me."

Alana laughed. "Yeah, I guess. But yours are in love with each other. Mine aren't."

"True enough."

"Do yours love each other?" Alana asked. "Really?"

"Honest answer? They love each other like sisters. I can't remember the last time I saw them kiss. Or hold hands. Or anything."

Alana shook her head. "I don't want that kind of marriage."

"To be married to a woman who loves you like a sister?" Zoey quipped. "I should say not. Unless you've switched teams lately."

"You know what I mean." Alana leaned back against her bed frame.

"Ah. You mean a spouse who's like a roommate. That would suck," Zoey agreed, then turned to face her. "Can I ask you something?"

"Sure."

"You have your mom's number at that place she's staying in Georgia?"

Alana nodded. "Yeah, but—"

"But nothing. I'm telling you, Alana. You need to call her before the wedding."

Alana thought back to the last time she'd tried calling her mother. How many months ago had it been? She couldn't remember. She did remember that her mother couldn't even come to the phone. That had been depressing. But this was depressing too.

She looked back at her friend. "Know what? I think you're right. I will."

CHAPTER SEVEN

One of Alana's favorite things to do in Las Vegas was to go incognito. As the daughter of Steve Skye, this was hard to make happen. She had one of the most recognizable faces in the city. However, she had learned from experience that if she picked her destinations carefully and dressed like a typical tourist, she might be overlooked and blend in with the crowd.

Dressing like a tourist meant putting on cutoff shorts, a T-shirt imprinted with the name of a Midwest state university like "Nebraska" or "Kansas State," flip-flops or no-name sneakers that she could buy at Big Lots, no makeup, and her dark hair back in a simple braid. This was her camouflage when she visited such downscale Vegas attractions as the free circus acts at the Circus

Circus Casino, the roller coaster at New York, New York, or even the vertigo-inducing rides at the top of the Stratosphere tower. Or, like the night after the first meeting with the wedding planner, when she went with Ellison to the Goretorium, the haunted house attraction right on the Strip.

The Goretorium had been built by the movie producer Eli Roth as an homage to his fascination with the bizarre and the bloody. The current Goretorium incarnation was of a hotel that had been taken over by cannibals. Called the Delmont Hotel, this was the last stop for gamblers who couldn't pay their bills, ne'er-do-wells, and various other denizens of the town who came in for the night and didn't ever come out.

Alana invited Ellison. Ellison had happily agreed to join her. They arrived separately to reduce any possibility that someone might spot them together and report to *Stripped* that they were dating. Like Alana, Ellison had dressed down. He wore a pair of baggy shorts and a Houseman University T-shirt.

Once they met up in the lobby, they bought admission tickets and waited with the masses for the tour to start. Alana looked forward to it. The Goretorium was supposed to be super-scary; a living environment that was more like a participation play than a museum. Roth had even hired

actors whose job was to don scary costumes and frighten the wits out of every visitor.

"I didn't even ask you. Are you a horror fan?" Alana asked Ellison. "You might hate all this stuff."

Ellison grinned. "Love horror. Edgar Allan Poe, H.P. Lovecraft, early Stephen King—more books than movies."

Alana had heard of Poe and King. Lovecraft, though, was new to her, and she said so.

"He wrote short stories about strange, repulsive, and bloodthirsty creatures," Ellison explained. "Want to hear one?"

"What?"

"I asked if you wanted to hear one. I have a bunch memorized," Ellison said.

"You do not have them memorized."

"Anything I read, I memorize," Ellison said with a shrug. "Listen. This is from the one called, 'The Nameless City.' " His voice dropped to horror-movie narrator depths; he used scary hand-gestures to underscore his words. " 'To convey any idea of these monstrosities is impossible. They were of the reptile kind, with body lines suggesting sometimes the crocodile, sometimes the seal, but more often nothing of which either the naturalist or the paleontologist ever heard.' " He smiled. "Like I said, memorized."

Alana's jaw dropped open. "How did you do that?"

"It's a blessing and a curse," Ellison told her. "Perfect recall. Same thing with conversations."

"You'd be a great detective. A one man CSI who doesn't forget anything. Like on that show *Unforgettable*. But real life."

"It's not so great," he confessed. "When I think back on life, I don't just remember the details. I remember the feelings. I kind of feel the feelings all over again. When I'm remembering good stuff, it's great. When it's not so good? It's painful."

The lobby was filling around them. It was a motley crew of American and international visitors. Alana heard English, Russian, Japanese, and French. The crowd was mostly families, though there was a group of five blonde teen girls from Norway. Not that Alana could pick out Norwegian, but the girls all wore matching T-shirts with the red, white, and blue Norwegian flag, plus the word "NORGE" in capital letters under the flag. Alana couldn't help but overhear their conversation, even as she mulled what Ellison was saying to her.

So many things would be easier with total recall. School. Winning an argument where someone claimed to have said X, but was now saying that they remembered Y. A person would never need to use GPS for directions—all they would need to do is look at a map once, and they'd

know a whole city. Learning a foreign language, like the Norwegian that the girls were speaking, would be a snap. What wouldn't be so good, she realized, was feeling all the emotions of an event like they were being felt for the first time.

When Alana had been told that her mother was not coming home from the hospital but instead was being transferred to the psych facility in Georgia, she had felt like she was dying. All the air had been blasted out of her lungs. Her heart had raced and slowed, raced and slowed. Bile riled her stomach, and the world had spun. As time passed, she could remember the event without feeling physically awful. Ellison didn't have that ability.

There was a flip side, though. The feelings of good memories would be there forever. A first kiss would always feel like a first kiss. Her own first kiss had been when she'd lived in New York, at Elliott Green's bar mitzvah, behind the curtains of the reception hall, with Elliott himself. She'd thought she was in love with Elliott. That kiss had left her lips more charged and buzzy than the shock that might come through an actual electric chair. She'd lost that feeling, though. All she could hope was that someday she'd have it again.

She'd come close to that feeling again in eleventh grade, when she and Cory had engaged in some fairly heavy duty

JEFF GOTTESFELD

petting. But her emotions were always tempered by her worries about herself. How much did he like her? Did he want to go further with her? How much further? And was she ready to go further, even if he wanted to?

She had the sense with him of being both inside herself and outside herself, looking at her own interactions like a scientist, even as she was living them. It was disconnected, and it wasn't so wonderful. She'd told herself countless times how great it had been to be Cory's girlfriend. However, now that he was making it obvious he wasn't interested in a relationship, she could see the problems they had back then more clearly.

Well. If he didn't want her, at least he wasn't hitting on any of her friends. That would have been difficult on every level. Seeing him with Zoey or Chalice ... ugh. She couldn't imagine how she'd deal with it.

Ellison touched her arm. "Listen to those girls." He indicated the Norwegians with his chin.

Alana listened more closely. They were clearly talking about Teen Tower. Alana didn't speak Norwegian, but "Teen Tower" was "Teen Tower" in every language. She decided to have some fun. That is, if the Norwegians spoke English.

"Excuse me?" She chose a strategic moment to interrupt. "Do you guys speak English?"

70

The tallest of the five girls, an athletic-looking blonde with hair down to her waist, nodded. "Of course. We all do."

"Great!" Alana exclaimed. "So, I couldn't help overhearing. You guys were talking about Teen Tower. Me and my friend here? Well, we're thinking about asking our parents to get us in."

Ellison nodded in agreement and played along. "For sure. But, you know, it's kind of expensive."

"It's *really, really* expensive," Alana mock-agreed. "So what we want to know is whether it's worth it. Is it?"

The girls all looked at her. Then they burst out laughing.

"Is it worth it? It's fantastic," the tall girl exclaimed.

"We've been there three days, one after another," said the shortest of the five. "And we're going back tomorrow."

"I wish we could be there right now!" declared a third girl.

Alana felt great to hear this. It was one thing to walk around Teen Tower talking to guests, but quite another to hear praise from strangers, who had no idea that the person they were talking to was the person in charge of the whole thing.

"That's … that's great to hear," she said, pleased.

"Hey, I got a question." Ellison's deep voice got the girls' attention. Or maybe it was his good looks. Or both.

"Yes?" the shortest girl asked.

"What do you know about Alana Skye? She's in charge of Teen Tower."

The tall girl spoke right up. "Well, everyone knows who she is, or at least knows about her. We didn't meet her, though. I wish I could. I think she's a genius. Everyone thinks she's a genius. I'd do anything to shake her hand."

"A genius, huh? That's good to know," Ellison said, and then he looked at Alana. "Well, the tour's about to start. See you around. Who knows? Maybe we'll see you at Teen Tower. And maybe one day you can meet Alana Skye."

"Yeah," Alana added. "I'd love to meet her too."

Ellison offered his hand; the girls all shook it. Then they offered their hands to Alana. She shook them, laughing inside. They would do anything to shake hands with Alana Skye. Little did they know they were in the process of doing just that.

Once the Goretorium tour began, it wasn't very long, but it was scary. They were ushered through a series of darkened rooms, full of the kinds of great props that would be found in the best horror movies. Walls of dismembered heads, torture devices in action, actors in bloodied clothes, caged people, and limbs detached from bodies were everywhere. There was even a real-life chainsaw

massacre carried out on a mannequin. At least, Alana
hoped the victim was a mannequin. Along the way, lights
flashed, sounds pulsated, and actors circulated through
the crowd, grabbing people and scaring them. By the time
they reached the last darkened room, the screaming had
reached an impossibly high pitch. When Alana found
herself grabbed, she hollered and leaped for the safety of
Ellison's arms. They enveloped her so warmly and safely
that she didn't want him to ever let go.

Then, the tour was over, and the crowd emptied into a
gift shop. Alana didn't want any souvenirs, but she did want
something to drink. Fortunately, there was a bar upstairs
that also served food, so all ages were welcome. The
cocktails—alcoholic and non-alcoholic—were all horror
themed, and the waitresses looked like they'd stepped out
of a Wes Craven movie. Plus, there was a surprisingly
good view of City Center through big windows. Ellison
led them to a table. They ordered drinks. A virgin "tortured
soul" for Alana, and a "bubbling eyeball" for Ellison.

"Non-alcoholic drink? I was sure you'd have a fake
ID," Ellison said.

Alana shook her head. "Actually, I don't."

"You and your friends don't sneak into nightclubs?"

"We don't sneak. Sometimes the bouncers let us in,
though. You're welcome to come with any time."

"We'd have to go public for that to happen," Ellison observed. "You ready for that?"

She looked at him and decided to be honest. Well, sort of honest. "Not really. Not yet."

"You let me know when you are, okay?"

Alana thought for a moment. When would be a good time to show the world that she was with Ellison? She knew almost instantly. "What are you doing Saturday night?"

"Nothing. But I think I'm about to be told I'm doing something."

She raised her glass to him. "You're right. It's my dad and Roxanne's wedding. I want you to be my date."

He clinked glasses with her. "Really? And what would your father say? Never mind, I accept. Provisionally."

"Provisionally?"

"Provisionally. If you and your boy pull it together by then? I'm good with that."

"You're unbelievable," she declared. "And I'm an adult. I don't care what my father would say."

"Nah, I'm not unbelievable. I just like to hang out with beautiful brunettes. I don't have a girlfriend now, so it's not an issue. Plus, I think I'm helping you, no?"

She grinned wickedly. "Yes."

WEDDING BELL BLUES

"Great."

They finished off their drinks and headed out of the Goretorium into the warm night air. Ready to go their separate ways, Alana had one last thing to say. "I know it's sort of dumb to say this since you can remember everything … but don't forget about our date."

CHAPTER EIGHT

By the time there were five days left until the wedding, Alana felt herself pulled in three directions. First, there was her regular work at Teen Tower. Second, the wedding planning with Zoey. Third was her secret friendship with Ellison. She was liking him more and more and was finding it harder and harder to keep it a secret.

She was astonished no one had picked up on how she was training with Ellison in the mornings, or her obvious efforts to visit the Teen Tower gym whenever she could. But somehow, she was keeping the depth of the relationship a secret, even from Zoey and Chalice. She was glad that by the wedding everything would be revealed. It seemed like the right time.

"How are things going with Cory?" Zoey asked. They

WEDDING BELL BLUES

were on their way to meet the wedding planner, the head hotel chef Jean-Claude Chanderot, and Roxanne. Abra had decided that Jean-Claude's kitchen would be best suited to turn out the fifteen hundred to two thousand dinners that would be served at the sit-down affair in the Desert Ballroom. They were going to sample the proposed menu. The tasting would be in Haiku, the hotel's Japanese sushi restaurant, which was normally only open for dinner.

"How's it going?" Alana answered, repeating Zoey's question back to her. "It goes slowly if at all, to tell the truth."

"Meaning, he's not all over the gorgeousness that is you?"

Alana laughed a little. "Hey. If he doesn't feel it, he doesn't feel it. I'm still here, I'm still standing, and I'll be okay. Cory or no Cory."

"That's frighteningly mature," Zoey opined. "You still want him, though."

Alana thought about that as they neared Haiku. Peering into the depths of her heart, she said, "True. But a girl doesn't always get what she wants."

"Tell me about it," Zoey declared. "Have you noticed how Chalice is hanging around with your assistant these days? She should be all over you like chips on a craps table. 'How can I help, Alana?' 'What can I do for you?

77

This has to be stressful for you, Alana.' 'Let's go to Nogi-zaka Hill Spa, Alana.' 'Alana, Alana, Alana.' "

Zoey's imitation of Chalice's high-pitched voice was so spot-on that Alana laughed heartily. Plus, she was making a good point. Chalice had been hanging around Kaylee a lot. In fact, ever since the wedding planning had started. In some ways it was good because Alana was spending less time on Teen Tower than Kaylee, and someone had to watch the operation during this run-up to the wedding. But in other ways it wasn't so good. It felt like Chalice was voting with her feet about her loyalty, and the vote was not for Alana.

Haiku's entrance was between the casino and the hotel lobby. Stepping inside was like stepping into another world. The restaurant was decorated in blue and white, with a white tile floor that gleamed so brightly Alana could practically see her reflection. The walls were covered with woodcut art. Quiet Gottan music was playing in the background. There was a variety of seating: both traditional Japanese tables at which diners could sit on the floor and conventional Western tables with chairs.

They found Roxanne and Abra at one of these tables with Jean-Claude. The chef was in whites with a toque—a tall chef's hat—while Roxanne wore a green shift dress, and Abra was in black jeans with a gray tunic.

WEDDING BELL BLUES

"Are we late?" Alana asked.

Roxanne shook her head. "You're fine. We're early. And we were just hearing some amazing news from Jean-Claude."

Abra nodded. "Even I think it's amazing, and I'm not easily amazed."

Alana and Zoey found seats; Jean-Claude passed them a menu that had been handwritten on fine rice paper.

"So here is my news," he told them as Alana scanned the menu. "I have just talked with your father, Alana. He wants to open a competitor to Mondrian. The hotel already has one four-star restaurant. He wants two. And the second one will bear my name: Chanderot."

"That's great," Alana told him, not sure what this had to do with the wedding. Then Roxanne filled her in.

"Jean-Claude wants the wedding party to eat what he plans to serve at Chanderot on opening night. And he wants us to try it now."

Jean-Claude signaled toward the kitchen. Five waiters in tuxedos came out carrying covered dishes. They put the covered dishes in front of the five of them, and then removed the tops with a flourish.

"We begin with toasted duck egg yolk, with salon eggs and herbs from the LV Skye garden," Jean-Claude announced.

79

Alana tasted it and practically swooned. It was spectacular. But the courses that followed were equally dazzling. There was a blueberry and roasted goat cheese salad with wasabi sorbet and minced tarragon. Spinach with wild mushrooms. Flash-cooked striped bass cheeks over a purée of kale. Monkfish filleted and seared. Then came the meat course, a roasted saddle of free-range buffalo with a fresh mint glaze. The meal finished with selections from a cheese cart and a roasted pear with warm chocolate sauce.

For a half hour, Alana, Zoey, and the others did nothing but eat. The portions were far smaller than would be served at the actual wedding dinner, since this was only a tasting session. Still, by the time they were done, Alana was more than full. She knew she'd just had one of the greatest meals of her life. If Jean-Claude could execute this menu for two thousand people instead of just five, it would be a wedding reception not quickly forgotten.

Abra had the same concern. "Jean-Claude, this was wonderful, but can you do this for a big crowd? And pair it with wine selections?"

Jean-Claude smiled. "Zoey's mothers will be asking that question the next day in their blog. How did Jean-Claude Chanderot do it?"

"They'll be there," Zoey assured him. "They might post about it right in the middle of the meal."

WEDDING BELL BLUES

Jean-Claude stood. "I look forward to that. Well then. My work is done, if the menu meets your approval?" He looked at Abra, not Roxanne.

Abra nodded, barely taking in Roxanne. "It does."

The chef nodded. "See you in the ballroom on Saturday night."

With no further ceremony, he headed for the kitchen, trailed by the five waiters. Abra announced that she had to go to the ballroom to check with the decorator—there was no reason for Roxanne to come along, and why didn't she just take a break. Zoey said she had to take care of a personal matter; she'd be back at Teen Tower in an hour. Both of them hurried off, leaving Roxanne and Alana alone in Haiku.

"Is this a set-up?" Roxanne joked.

"For me to be alone with my future stepmother? Hard to believe."

There was a teapot filled with green tea on the table. Roxanne poured some for herself, and then filled Alana's cup.

"What's this like for you?" Roxanne asked.

"Excuse me?"

Roxanne sipped her tea. "Your father getting married again. Your father getting married to me. This big affair, with all this attention. Your being asked to help with a

81

wedding that you might not even think is a good idea. I don't know a better way to ask it. What's it like?"

Alana's first thought was that this was some sort of a trap. How could she be sure that whatever she told Roxanne would not be repeated to her father? Was Roxanne trying to bond with her for real, or was this just her way to suck out some information that Alana's father would want to know?

She wondered what Zoey would advise her to do. She knew the answer. Zoey would say to be cautious. Super-duper cautious. Alana didn't really know this woman from Adam. Or Eve, as it were. And what would Kaylee, who had such good judgment, counsel her to say? Kaylee would probably say to give Roxanne part of the truth, a part that didn't make much difference, and see if it got repeated to Steve. If it didn't get repeated, Alana could tell Roxanne more later, but only if it felt right.

Alana decided to combine the approaches. "I appreciate the question, even if I'm not so comfortable with it."

Roxanne smiled. "Why would you be? You barely know me."

"It's not just that." Time for the partial truth. "I already have a mother. I'm not sure I need a second one."

"Interesting. I was kind of in the same situation as you once upon a time, you know," Roxanne related.

82

WEDDING BELL BLUES

"What do you mean?" Alana sipped her tea as Roxanne seemed to compose her thoughts.

"My parents divorced when I was in college. I was a little older than you, but not much. My father never remarried, but my mother got married eighteen months later. Eighteen months! You know what that made me think?"

Alana nodded. "Yup. Affair."

"Exactly," Roxanne echoed Alana. "And hey—I'm not telling you anything that I haven't said to my mom, so don't think I'm spreading gossip." Her future stepmother put down her tea. "I couldn't help feeling betrayed, even though it had been my father who was betrayed."

"Did you go to the wedding?" Alana asked.

"Well, I didn't want to—" Roxanne peered at her. "Are you considering not coming to the wedding?"

Alana hadn't had that thought … until now.

"I don't know," she confessed as she considered it. "I'll probably be there, out of respect for my dad."

"But not out of respect for me," Roxanne surmised.

Alana shrugged. "I don't know you. I mean—okay, I'm just going to ask this—isn't this kind of sudden for you to want to marry him?"

"I wonder if you should turn that question around," Roxanne said. "Isn't it kind of sudden for your dad to want

to marry me? He asked me, after all. It totally caught me off guard."

Well. That was interesting. It sounded like this wedding was Steve's idea. Alana checked her cell. She had to get back to Teen Tower. She had a call she needed to make before she went. "I've gotta go. Can I ask you one more thing?"

Roxanne nodded. "Sure. Ask away."

"What did your dad think of your mom getting remarried? And what did you think of it?"

"That's two questions," Roxanne pointed out. "But I'll answer them. My father didn't care. If someone else wanted to be stuck with my mom, that was their choice. You'll see them be nice to each other at the wedding, probably, but he hates her now. Me? I was against it at first. Ten years later? What can I say? She's happier now than I'd ever seen her with my dad." Roxanne stood. "Come on. I'll walk you out."

They stepped across the gleaming floor to the door, and Roxanne opened it. "Look, Alana. I'm not asking you to make me your new mom. But I think you'll find, if you give me a chance, we could be friends. Thanks for talking."

Roxanne left. Alana stayed in the Haiku foyer near the carved wood front desk where guests usually waited to be seated. She sat on one of the plush white leather chairs and

took out her cell. There was indeed a call she had to make. She hadn't used the contact in a long time, but it was still on her phone. One touch and she was through. Her call was answered on the first ring.

"Oakmont Psychiatric," the voice at the other end said.

"May I speak to Carli Warshaw Skye, please? She's a patient. This is her daughter, Alana. I'm on her call list."

"Do you have your challenge code, Alana?"

Alana touched another button on her iPhone and read off a series of seemingly random numbers. This was the challenge code the facility had given her to prove that she was who she said she was.

"Okay, Alana. Stand by. Let's see if she'll come to the phone."

Alana waited. And waited. And waited. It had been so hard to make this call. What would she even say when her mother came to the phone?

She didn't have to worry about that. After what felt like an eternity, she heard the operator's voice. "I'm sorry, Carli Warshaw Skye is not available for a phone call."

Alana felt heartsick. "Did you tell her it was her daughter?"

"I'm sorry, she's not available," the operator repeated.

"What if I try later?" Making this call had been so hard. To be stymied now …

JEFF GOTTESFELD

"I'm sorry. She's not available. That's all I'm authorized to say. Have a nice day."

The operator clicked off. Alana had a moment where she was ready to stamp her heel through her phone. Then that moment was gone. All she could do was sit blankly, her heart as empty as the rest of Haiku.

CHAPTER NINE

"Hey, Boo, what's up today?"

"Big meeting," Alana texted back. "Starting soon."

"About?"

"Top secret, for time being."

"You holding out on me?"

Alana smiled. Ellison was always so precise with his language and speaking in person. That he got slangy and street in his texts was an endless source of amusement for her. She wondered if he did it with everyone or just with her. All she had to do was ask him. With his memory, he'd certainly remember. Of course, if she did ask him, she'd have to hear an answer that might be disappointing.

"No holdout. News at 11."

"Roger that. But I'm gonna keep bugging you. U mind?"

Alana smiled again. Mind? She didn't mind at all.

"Nah. Love it."

"Bug, bug, bug. CU l8r."

Alana didn't text Ellison back. She'd actually seen him just about an hour ago when she was down in the Teen Tower gym for another one-on-one training session. Ellison was right. Though she was sore in places that she didn't know could get sore, she could already start to see herself toning up, especially in her triceps and abs. Even better, she'd already dropped three pounds. If she got those kinds of results in less than a week, what would it be like if she trained with him for the whole summer? She couldn't wait to find out. It had been four or five days in a row now, and no one had seen them in the gym. It was one of the advantages to working out so early.

Alana anticipated another hellacious day at Teen Tower. She'd awakened to a story in *Stripped* about the wedding. How various celebrities were vying with each other to get better and more spectacular gifts for the happy couple. Then she'd read and watched some cell phone video about how Phantom had performed at the Las Vegas 51's Minor League Baseball stadium, and someone

WEDDING BELL BLUES

had tried to unmask him. The situation had apparently gotten ugly and a little dangerous. A witness reported that Phantom and his assistant had fled the scene.

Alana knew full well who that assistant was. Kaylee. She didn't like it one bit. She'd told Kaylee she could work with Reavis as long as it didn't interfere with her work at Teen Tower. If she and Reavis found themselves at the center of a mob, or even worse, arrested, that would be what Alana defined as "interfering with her work."

She opened her e-mail to send a warning note to Kaylee but saw that Kaylee had already sent one to her:

To: Alana
From: Kaylee
Re: Phantom

Hey and good morning. Hope all is good. Did you read about Reavis's show last night at the ballpark? Disaster, almost. We got away, but he was nearly unmasked and beaten up too. It's in *Stripped*. So listen, I think I've finally convinced Reavis that he needs to talk to your father about a regular gig. I want him at Teen Tower every day as a closing act, and I think you do too. No way this happens without your dad. I'm sure your dad

is full-frontal busy with the wedding, but I think
we should do the meeting f-a-s-t before Reavis
changes his mind. Can you set it up?

-K

Alana called Mrs. Rogers, her father's secretary, who
was like the female version of Mr. Clermont. She was
always on duty and never seemed to sleep. Fortunately,
her father had an opening at ten o'clock. Mrs. Rogers set
up the meeting. Then Alana had advised Kaylee, who said
she'd be there with Reavis. The meeting would take place
in Steve's conference room. They all agreed to rendezvous
at fifteen minutes before.

There was, however, someone else whom Alana wanted
in that meeting. Someone who, in her opinion, had earned
the right to be there. Zoey. She'd been such a great friend
since Alana had brought her on to work at Teen Tower and
to help with the wedding. She'd texted Zoey, who happily
said she'd come. Then she texted Cory since he also knew
Phantom's secret identity. He'd be useful at the meeting
too since Steve knew him well.

Zoey arrived forty-five minutes before the meeting.
The two of them decided to walk through one of the hotel's
indoor tropical gardens before heading to Alana's dad's
office. Those gardens had all kinds of tropical plants, trees,

and even parrots and non-poisonous snakes. To enter and exit, one had to step through an air lock into the controlled environment of the greenhouse. The gardens were only open to the public for a couple of hours a day, the better to protect the flora and fauna.

"What's the big mystery?" Zoey asked when they'd entered through the air lock. "Sounds like the whole world is gonna be in your dad's office. Seriously. Thanks for asking me. What's it about?"

"If this doesn't work out," Alana said to her, "you have to promise not to spill to your mothers."

"Sure, sure, you keep saying that about everything, you know," Zoey told her as they stopped under a huge joy perfume tree. Five hyacinth macaws cavorted in the branches above, as if they were still in the rain forest. "You have my word. But it would help to know what I'm not supposed to spill about."

"Cool. Okay. Here it is." Alana hesitated for a moment. She knew Kaylee wouldn't be happy with her bringing Zoey into the secret about Phantom without discussing it first. But, hey. She was the boss. She had to do what she thought was best for Teen Tower. "I know who Phantom is."

Zoey made a face. "Duh. Of course you know who he is. He performed here on opening day, remember? You've

been keeping it a secret all this time. And me? I'm such a good friend I haven't even asked you about it. And don't think my moms haven't been all up in my stuff. Because they have."

Alana was about to say more when a text came in.

"Hey, Boo, bug u bug u bug u."

She smiled. Ellison.

"All good, just working."

"Who's that? Cory?" Zoey asked.

Alana nodded, not wanting to get into the whole Ellison-Cory thing right now with Zoey. She needed more time. "Yep."

"When I gonna b able 2 bug u in person?"

Alana's fingers flew over the letters of her phone.

"Sneak out lunch? Will keep u posted."

Then a text did come in from Cory.

"Running a little late, 9:50."

"NP," she texted back as another one came from Ellison.

"Don't need eats, need u."

She grinned and typed back, **"KK."**

"He's keeping you busy," Zoey observed.

Her cell sounded again with an incoming text from Ellison, **"Counting mins."**

"And I'm counting seconds."

WEDDING BELL BLUES

Then her cell sounded one more time. Text from Cory.
"What? Counting seconds? I just said I'd be a little late!"

Alana blanched. She thought she'd been writing Ellison. She realized how close to disaster she'd just been.

She typed in, **"Just joking,"** and hoped that would be the end of it. Since neither Cory nor Ellison texted her back, it seemed to be. Thank God.

"What was I saying?" Alana turned back to Zoey, who was distracted by a Vietnamese mossy frog that had hopped out of the garden's brook and was now staring at them from the middle of the path.

"That if you kiss that frog, he'll turn into Cory," Zoey joked.

"No, seriously."

They started walking again, stepping gingerly past the frog. "Before you were so rudely interrupted, you were saying something about Phantom."

"That's right. So, listen. He's finally ready to do a gig here at Teen Tower. We have to convince my father to make it happen. That's what this meeting is about. I need your help."

"Shouldn't be hard, he's the bomb. The whole city wants him."

"Yeah. That's what I think too."

93

JEFF GOTTESFELD

Zoey bent to smell some frangipani blooms growing in a small pond close to the path. "Well, we'll just have to make Steve a believer. He saw him at the opening. And I've seen him perform twice now. I'm a believer."

Alana checked her cell. "That's why I'm going to let you speak first. He's expecting me to start, but you can talk about the Phantom buzz and what we saw. I know I was there too, but my dad will listen to you before he'll listen to me on this."

"That works. Anything else going on I should know? Other than our friend Chalice turning into Kaylee's little redheaded shadow?" Zoey declared.

Alana realized she hadn't told Zoey about her attempt to call her mother in Georgia.

"I took your advice, you know," Alana said softly.

"Which part? I give so much of it, and it's all so good."

"I tried to call my mom."

Zoey turned to face her, her eyes more open and welcoming than Alana had ever seen. "Good for you." Her voice was as soft as Alana's. "What happened?"

"It's what didn't happen," Alana muttered. "She didn't even come to the phone."

"Hey. Maybe there was a good reason. Was she sleeping? Walking around the grounds? With a psychiatrist? What did they tell you?"

94

Alana shook her head. "They didn't tell me anything. Just that she wasn't available."

Zoey put an arm around her shoulder. "I'm proud of you. That took a lot of guts. You can try again sometime."

Alana felt her body shrink a little. "I don't know if I can try again. It took a lot out of me just to do it that once."

"Got it. Whatever you decide, I'm with you. Come on." Zoey squeezed Alana's shoulder. "We've got a meeting to nail."

They left the garden and walked together to the business wing of the hotel. As usual, her father's executive assistant, Mrs. Rogers, greeted her bluntly. Mrs. Rogers was known for her efficiency, not for her looks or her warmth. Cory was there already—clearly he hadn't needed the extra time. His greeting was polite and friendly but not effusive. Alana saw Zoey raise her eyebrows at that. Then Kaylee and Reavis entered together. Reavis was actually wearing his Phantom mask.

Kaylee looked at Alana sharply as soon as she noticed Zoey.

"Can we talk?" Kaylee asked.

"We are talking," Alana said smoothly.

"I mean privately."

Alana looked at Mrs. Rogers, who pointed to the clock.

JEFF GOTTESFELD

"If you're all here, your dad may want you in at any time. Don't go far."

"Fine," Alana said. She'd sort of expected this.

Together, they stepped outside into the corridor.

"What is she doing here?" Kaylee demanded.

"Zoey?"

"No," Kaylee said. "Justin Bieber in drag. Of course Zoey!"

Alana took a deep breath. "I'm in charge of Teen Tower. I thought it would help our case to have her here with us. We'll find out soon if I'm right."

"If Zoey knows who Phantom is—that it's Reavis. She'll go to her moms. They'll put it in the blog, and then the whole secret-identity thing will get wrecked!"

Alana had never seen Kaylee this upset. What's more, she didn't think it was justified. "Look," she told Kaylee. "You may be good at the hospitality business, but you don't know my father like I do. If you want Reavis to get hired, you want Zoey in this meeting. If you don't, then you don't. It's as simple as that."

"She better not wreck it," Kaylee said crossly.

Alana fumed. Who was Kaylee to talk about wrecking it or not? And why would Kaylee think that Alana would invite Zoey along if Zoey was going to wreck things?

96

Then Mrs. Rogers stuck her head into the hall. "Your dad's ready for you," she told them.

"Okay," Alana said. "We're coming."

As they headed toward the conference room, Alana could cut the tension with Kaylee with a knife, but she was sure she was doing the right thing. The next half hour would tell her whether she was right, or absolutely, completely, brutally wrong.

CHAPTER TEN

They filed into the conference room. Steve's huge, custom-made leather chair was always on the side closest to the door. They were to sit on the other side of the massive wooden conference table. Alana sat first, with Zoey and Reavis to one side of her. Cory and Kaylee took the other side. Though the secretary had said that Steve was ready for them, they had to wait a couple of minutes for him to return from whatever he'd been doing. He addressed them as he took his seat.

"You called this meeting, Alana. Start it. But I'm a busy man, and I'm getting married this weekend. You've got fifteen minutes."

As they'd discussed, Alana turned to Zoey. "Why don't you tell my dad why we're here?"

WEDDING BELL BLUES

"Thanks, Alana," Zoey said as Alana chanced a glance over at Kaylee. Her assistant's eyes darkened. Alana realized anew that she was more hurt by Zoey's attendance than Alana had intended for her to be. Well, too late to do anything about that now. The plane had taken off. If Kaylee hadn't been so confrontational a few minutes before, Alana knew she would have had time to share her careful plan for how the meeting would unfold.

"Let me say first to Alana," Zoey started, "what an honor it has been to work for you during these last few days. Because of your dad's wedding, you've been busier than any girl should be. I'm delighted to have been able to step in and take up some of the slack. It's been a thrill for me."

"You're welcome," Alana said.

Steve cleared his throat and made a move-it-along gesture with his right hand. "Cut to the chase and end the lovefest, girls. You didn't come here to slather makeup on each other."

"No, we didn't," Zoey said directly. "We're here because we have a chance to hire the hottest magician in town to come and work at Teen Tower. You've read about Phantom in my moms' blog. He's this guerilla magician. Hit and run. At Penn and Teller's show. Then at the Palms where I filmed him. Then he walked on water at Treasure

99

JEFF GOTTESFELD

Island. The Teen Tower opening, of course. And finally he did this thing at the ballpark … for which, I must say, his assistant looked a lot like Kaylee Ryan. I'm just saying."

Steve nodded. He'd been there for the Teen Tower opening and had seen Phantom wow the crowd. "I've seen the video from last night. Your moms posted it. If I have an issue with Alana's assistant, I'll take it up with Alana and her assistant, thank you very much."

"Fair enough," Zoey acknowledged. "Excuse me." She poured herself some water, then plunged ahead. Alana thought she was doing a great job. It was exactly what she'd wanted. "Thank you. So, to continue, Phantom is the magician the whole city is talking about. Phantom is doing tricks that no one else can do. Phantom has the goods and the attitude. He has mystery. He'll bring even more people to Teen Tower. Alana and I are proposing that he work every evening right before closing, a half-hour show at the Teen Tower main stage."

Steve sat back in his leather chair, stretched out his arms, and then folded them. When he talked again, he directed his words to Cory of all people.

"Cory, what do you think?" Steve asked.

"I'm in favor, sir," Cory told him.

Just the sound of his voice made Alana's stomach do flips. She felt a pang of longing. She'd been trying

100

to squelch down her feelings for him. It was impossible. There was still a core of her that wanted him more than she'd ever wanted anyone.

"You agree with everything?"

"With everything. I have to say, I've never heard as much buzz about a magician since Criss Angel got started. Or maybe David Blaine. I think if you hire Phantom, this could be the start of a franchise."

Well, that helped and hurt at the same time. It was good to get her father thinking about a franchise. It was painful to be in the same room with Cory and hear him speak.

Steve shifted his body in Kaylee's direction. "What about you, Kaylee? Or does your special relationship with Phantom mean you can't be objective?"

Kaylee seemed taken aback by the question. Reavis jumped in to answer for her. "She doesn't have a special relationship with me. She helps with my tricks. That's all."

"When I'm ready to talk to you, I'll talk to you, Reavis. Now, Kaylee? I asked you a question."

Whoa. Alana breathed in hard. Steve knew Reavis's name. But how? She looked at her father. The corners of his lips curled into a knowing smile that he always got when he could show off that he knew more than people thought he knew. Alana had seen that smile a lot in her eighteen years.

JEFF GOTTESFELD

Unmasked, as it were, Reavis took off his mask and laid it on the table in front of them.

"We meet again," Steve said to him.

"Yes we do," Reavis responded.

"You're a better magician now, I understand."

"Yes, sir. I believe I am," Reavis agreed.

"How did you find out his real name?" Kaylee cut in, completely dodging Steve's original question.

Steve laughed. "Oh, please. I've known since he did that mystery show at the Teen Tower opening with you."

"But how?"

Steve pushed some buttons on a small console in front of his place at the conference table. The room darkened. At the same time, a photograph displayed on one of the big screens. It was a Toyota RAV4 from the back. Alana could see it had Texas license plates. "This is a digression, Kaylee, but since you asked. We take photos of every vehicle coming in and out of our parking lot. After opening day, we looked at all the cars coming and going from Teen Tower. Once we identified the car, it was no problem to trace the plates."

He brought the lights back up and regarded Reavis. "You have to do better on your misdirection." Then he took in Kaylee again. "You agree that I should make Reavis a headliner?"

102

"Yes, sir. With all my heart. And I won't have to risk my life helping him with his tricks ever again."

Everyone laughed, even her father. Alana saw Cory look at Kaylee with appreciation for the tension-cutting remark. She wished he would look at her that way just once.

"I promise, Kaylee, that I'll have a different assistant," Reavis quipped.

"Not so fast," Steve declared, indicating that Reavis didn't have the job just yet. "Everyone, you need to watch this."

He dimmed the lights and pressed another button. This time, a video played with a time and date stamp from two years ago.

It was Reavis. A little younger, a little thinner, but still him. And he was doing magic tricks in this same conference room for her father. That her dad would be auditioning people was no shocker. He probably auditioned fifty people for every entertainment opening at the LV Skye. But that he had auditioned Reavis before; that was the real shocker. Kaylee hadn't mentioned it to her. Did she know about this?

Yes, Alana decided. She surely had to have known. She should have said something.

Alana clutched her chair as she watched the audition.

103

JEFF GOTTESFELD

Reavis was no better in this audition than a mediocre magician at a birthday party. Actually, he was worse. He dropped cards. He dropped balls. Baby chickens pooped in his hands. His patter was nervous; the execution worse. Alana realized that if she was her father, she wouldn't have hired this guy to wash dishes.

Steve played the tape all the way through, until it went black. "That's the great Reavis in this very room two years ago," her dad said once the lights were up again.

"I'm better than that now, sir," Reavis responded.

"That might be true," Steve acknowledged. "I saw you on opening day, and I've seen the clips from the last few weeks. Damned impressive."

"Thank you, sir."

"You're welcome. But the fact remains, you cracked when you auditioned for me before. Which scares me. And I don't like to be scared."

Kaylee spoke up for her friend. "He's different now."

"No!" Steve thundered. "He's the same magician with more experience. But his heart is the same."

Her father sat silently for a moment. He checked his watch, sighed, and then seemed to make a decision. But first he looked at Alana. His eyes seemed to say, *I'm doing this for you. Don't forget that.* Then he fixed his gaze on Reavis again. "You brought some of your act with you?"

104

WEDDING BELL BLUES

Reavis nodded that he did.

"Give us a trick. And put your mask back on. I like that Phantom thing," Steve instructed. "Go."

Reavis reached for the mask he'd laid on the table and put it back on. Then he moved to the open area at the far end of the conference table. He wore a black sport jacket over his black shirt and trousers—in the right pocket were several small balls of many different colors. He started to juggle those balls, bouncing them off his elbows, knees, even his nose. It was dazzling.

Then it stopped being dazzling. A pink ball fell to the floor and rolled away. And then a red one.

"I'm sorry," Reavis muttered.

Alana winced with embarrassment both for him and for herself. This was like an instant replay of the audition he'd done for Steve two years ago, only worse, because he'd had two extra years to prepare for this one. There was really no excuse. Did the guy have a professional death wish or something?

Alana looked at Kaylee, who seemed sick to her stomach. Alana wasn't upset. She was angry. Even this audition was making her look bad in her father's eyes. What would he think the next time she asked for a meeting with him during a time when he was ridiculously busy?

"More," he called to Reavis.

105

Reavis seemed to pull himself together and found a deck of cards in the left front jacket pocket. "I'm going to do the same card trick as two years ago."

He started shuffling the cards. It was a shuffling clinic. Cards slid up his arm and down his arm back into the deck. He cut the deck into halves, then quarters, then eighths. He shuffled behind his back. He shuffled so that cards flew six inches from one hand into another. It was so fantastic that Alana felt ready to applaud. Zoey was nodding approvingly. Kaylee beamed. Alana saw the future. Her father was going to offer this guy a gig, and he was going to become the Next Big Thing. Knowing her dad, he'd sign Reavis to a long-term contract. People wouldn't think of the LV Skye without thinking of Phantom. They wouldn't think of Phantom without thinking of—

Oh no.

In the middle of a spectacular shuffle, the devil of magic intervened. Instead of the cards settling in Reavis's hands again, they flew out like they'd been shot from a cannon—like the world's biggest game of 52-Pickup. There were cards everywhere. On the floor. On the table. In people's laps. Disaster. The air went out of Reavis like a blimp hit by an antiaircraft missile. It was a crash and burn of epic proportions. In fact, he'd managed to top his humiliation of two years ago.

WEDDING BELL BLUES

"Reavis," Steve said with cutting directness, "you can spare yourself a lot of embarrassment if you'd just leave now. And don't come back. You obviously haven't gotten your nerves together in two years of prep. Maybe you can work birthday parties."

Reavis appeared calm. He didn't move. Instead, he pointed to the table in front of Steve.

"There's a card in front of you, Mr. Skye."

Steve took in the facedown card. "I can see that."

"If I didn't know better, I'd say it was the ace of hearts. But it's facedown, so I couldn't know better. But maybe you know better. Can you turn it over please?"

Whoa. Was this part of the trick? Alana felt Zoey poke her in the ribs. She understood too. Maybe those flying cards hadn't been random. Maybe, just maybe …

Steve flipped the card and held it aloft so Alana and the others could see. It was, indeed, an ace. But it was the ace of spades.

Alana sighed loudly. Everyone else fidgeted. It would have been so cool if …

"Oops," Reavis declared. "Wrong card. I meant the one in your lap."

Steve reached down. Alana couldn't see his lap, of course, but there was a card there. He held it aloft.

Holy holy holy. It was the ace of hearts.

107

JEFF GOTTESFELD

"How'd you do that?" Steve demanded.

"Skills, sir."

"That is an impossible trick!"

Reavis grinned. "And yet I made it happen."

Steve stood. "Meeting's over. I'll let you know."

He strode out of the room. Kaylee and Cory waited for Reavis to gather up his cards. The three left together. Only Alana and Zoey remained.

"What do you think?" Alana asked her friend.

"I think that last trick was fantastic. And I think that if he hadn't dropped the balls, literally, your dad would have given him the job right then and there," Zoey said. "You know how he did it, don't you?"

Alana shook her head. "No clue."

"Well, I can't prove it. But I think those cards were marked on the back in some special way. He could tell from their backs what was on the face."

That made sense … except for the card in her dad's lap. How could he possibly have seen that one?

"Dunno," Zoey admitted after Alana voiced what she was thinking. "Maybe he guessed."

"Or maybe he's just the best magician in the country, and we need him at Teen Tower."

They were about to leave together when the conference room door opened. Alana thought it might be her dad, or

108

WEDDING BELL BLUES

Mrs. Rogers, or someone else who had a meeting scheduled there. It was none of the above. To her surprise, it was Roxanne. She had on a simple yellow sundress and carried a small shopping bag. For the first time, it seemed, Alana was seeing her without makeup. She looked younger than her twenty-eight years.

"Hi," Roxanne said, almost shyly.

"Hi," Alana greeted her. Zoey offered a polite nod.

"I … I brought you something," Roxanne said. She put the shopping bag on the table and took out a small wrapped gift. "Here. For you. A wedding present. I know it's not normal for the bride to give the groom's daughter a present, but there's nothing normal about this wedding, is there? Anyway, I hope you like it. Maybe you'll even wear it on Saturday night."

Alana stared at the gift. It was beautifully wrapped in silver paper with a white bow. The gift was thoughtful, but it also made her uncomfortable. Its very existence meant that Roxanne had to have been thinking about her.

"Um, Alana?" Zoey asked. "When someone gives you a present, the customary thing to do is open it."

"Yes. You're right, Zoey," agreed Roxanne.

Alana moved to the table and unwrapped the gift. A jewelry box, obviously, once she got the wrapping paper off. She opened it.

109

"Wow," she breathed despite her best efforts to stay cool.

Inside the box was a platinum letter *A* outlined in sapphires with a platinum wrist-length chain. It was exquisite. Since Alana was already thinking of wearing a sleeveless dress to the wedding, the bracelet would work wonderfully.

"You like?"

Alana nodded.

Zoey took the case from her hands. "Let's get this mother on you."

Zoey took the charm from the box and fastened the chain around Alana's left wrist. Though the lighting in the conference room was better suited for work than for beauty, it still looked breathtaking. "It looks great," Zoey declared.

Alana turned to Roxanne. "Thank you. This is … this is very meaningful."

"I'm glad you think so."

There was no reason for it to be meaningful. Alana had more jewelry than most women three times her age. Roxanne had plenty of money. Though the piece had to be pricey by normal standards, there was nothing normal about Roxanne's bank account. No. It was the effort. It

was that Roxanne had planned this, executed this, and delivered this. That impressed Alana a lot. For the first time, she started to think that there could be worse stepmothers in the world than Roxanne Hunter-Gibson.

CHAPTER ELEVEN

Mornings were turning into Alana's favorite time of day. It was when she woke up early, put on her workout gear, and met Ellison in the Teen Tower gym. As the week wore on, they started their workout session earlier and earlier. First, they'd train at seven thirty. Then, seven. And then they cranked it back to six thirty. Alana told herself it was so she'd have more time to go through her routine.

In truth, she knew it was so she could spend more time with Ellison. He was so easy to be around. Strong, wise, and funny. That total recall thing with the memory was weird. Alana wondered if it meant that he had total recall of every moment with every girl he'd ever kissed. Probably. Which meant that Ellison was not the right guy to ask about his past girlfriends. It was also intimidating

because maybe it meant every person that Ellison kissed was being held up against a memory of all the girls he'd kissed before. Did he have some kind of mental ranking system of hotness? A pie chart? A bar graph of hot kisses?

It was a bad thought. Ellison had never mentioned a previous girlfriend, though it was impossible to believe a great guy like him hadn't had a girlfriend in his past. Probably more than one. So far, she'd been able to adhere to a "don't ask, don't tell" policy. She didn't ask, and he didn't tell.

The morning after the meeting with her dad about Reavis, Alana was out of the penthouse by six fifteen. Mr. Clermont was on duty already, smiled approvingly, and reported that Steve was pleased with Alana's new regimen. It indicated self-discipline. Alana was pleased with it too, and not just because her triceps looked better than ever.

By now, her routine was set: fifteen minutes of abdominals, then isolation work on two muscle groups, and then thirty minutes of cardio. Alana used the time to debrief with Ellison about what was going on in her life and about the wedding. That morning she filled him in on the previous day's meeting with Phantom.

"What do you think your dad's going to do?" he asked as he guided her through a set of glute squats with his hands on her hips. Alana liked that part.

"Not sure," she told him. "That's my dad. He'll let people twist in the wind just for the fun of it."

"My father's the same way," Ellison told her. "He intimidates the hell out of his lower-division classes."

"Tough love," Alana said as she worked through another set. She could feel the heat from his hand on her hip.

Then the set was over. "You're getting stronger," Ellison said.

"Thanks," Alana said. She was beaming.

"I wonder if this would help you. Or hurt you."

He put his hands on her shoulders. She didn't resist. He kissed her. The kiss was soft but intense. He didn't pull her to his body like so many guys might have. Instead, he let his lips do the talking. She talked back. It was a wonderful conversation.

The kiss was still in progress when Alana heard a loud crashing noise. Clattering metal, like someone had knocked over a trash can. They broke apart and looked toward the sound. There, at the entrance to the gym, was a trash can in the middle of the floor. Standing frozen fifteen feet from the trash can was a blonde girl.

No doubt about it. It was Kaylee Ryan.

Alana cursed. She and Kaylee stared across the expanse of the gym at each other. Then Alana turned back to Ellison.

"Come on," she said softly. "We need to talk to her."

Alana felt bad. Here Kaylee had been trying to buff her up to Cory, and then she walks in on Ellison and her kissing. She had to feel betrayed.

"Hi," Kaylee said when they all met near the elliptical machines. "I didn't expect that anyone would be here."

"We're … training. I've been training Alana for a while now," Ellison chimed in.

Alana winced a little. They had been doing more than training. If all Kaylee had seen was them training, they wouldn't be having this discussion.

"I can see that. I was going to work out too. But I think maybe we need to talk, Alana. Don't you?"

Alana nodded to Kaylee. Things might have been a little rocky with Kaylee lately because of how Zoey had become so indispensable in this run-up to the wedding, but Kaylee was still her assistant. Plus, she liked her. She faced Ellison. "Let me talk with Kaylee. If I have time, I'll come back and finish up."

"Sounds good. I'm going to work my pecs," Ellison told her. He took a few steps away, then turned and jogged toward the dumbbells and benches in the rear of the gym.

Alana tried a joke. "So, you turning into a gym rat?"

"No," Kaylee replied flatly.

"Uh, I just wondered if you'd started coming to the

115

gym a lot lately. So, um, yeah. I'm training with Ellison. How much did you see?"

She hoped against hope that Kaylee hadn't seen the kiss. That hope was dashed when Kaylee made a kissing shape with her lips.

"Okay. So you saw."

"I saw." Kaylee nodded.

"We like each other. What can I tell you?"

Alana knew she sounded defensive, but couldn't Kaylee understand that she was under an incredible amount of pressure these days? She was planning to tell Kaylee on her own time. There was a limit to what a person could juggle. Where was Kaylee's gratitude for how Alana had hired her in the first place, and for how Kaylee didn't have to worry about her crazy aunt anymore? That could have been a real mess, but Alana had taken care of it so the aunt couldn't come to the hotel and bother her.

Kaylee was livid. "I thought you liked Cory. I was helping you to like Cory. Or to get Cory to like you. Or something like that."

"I do like Cory," Alana told her. "Stand by." She got some cold water from the cooler and returned with a softer attitude. Kaylee seemed to have calmed herself too. "But Cory's not into me. Why, I don't know. Meanwhile, Ellison is a great guy, right? Right?"

WEDDING BELL BLUES

"Yeah. He's cool. But ..."

"What?"

"I think you have to be straight up with Cory. Tell him what's going on," Kaylee said.

Alana knew that Kaylee was right. If she was going to be hanging with Ellison, she should tell Cory that. Who knows? She hadn't known Cory to be a jealous guy, but maybe the sight of her with Ellison would be enough to make him come back after her. A girl could certainly hope. "Okay. You're right. I will. Anything else?"

"Yeah," Kaylee said. "There is one more thing."

"What's that? And then I'll go finish my workout." Alana felt a lot better to have things straight with Kaylee. Plus, she liked the idea of making Cory jealous by seeing her with Ellison. Maybe Cory would see them dancing at the wedding, come over, and cut in. That would be sweet. "Three days to the wedding, you know. I have to look great."

"You may not like this ..."

"What?" Honestly. Kaylee could take so long to get to the point.

"Well, if you're with Ellison, I guess it's not a problem. I think Cory and I like each other. A lot."

Holy wow. Cory was into Kaylee, and Kaylee was into Cory. Had the universe turned inside out? Alana was infuriated by this news. At Cory. At Kaylee. At the world.

117

JEFF GOTTESFELD

Do not let on that you're ticked, Alana told herself silently. *Control yourself. Control yourself.*

"Good luck with him. He's a great guy. You should be with a great guy."

"You're not … you're not mad?" Kaylee asked.

Somehow, Alana managed a smile. "Mad? About what?"

"Great!" Kaylee exclaimed. She threw her arms around Alana.

It felt like the hug from hell.

CHAPTER TWELVE

Alana? I got your text. You needed to talk to me?"

Alana looked up. There was Cory. She had been alone in the Teen Tower office. Kaylee was handling a crisis in the dining room and wouldn't be back for a while. This was the perfect time to have the conversation with Cory that needed to happen; the one she'd promised Kaylee she would have.

At least she'd had a few hours to decide what she wanted to say. She had three things to think about: the short-, medium-, and long-term. Her father always said that too many people worry about the short term without thinking about the medium or long. Alana was ready to endure some short-term pain if it meant medium- and long-term gain.

JEFF GOTTESFELD

She nodded at Cory and indicated the empty seat by Kaylee's desk. "Yeah. Have a seat."

"Is there a problem with Teen Tower social media?" He sat. "Because if there is, I can fix it."

"Nope. No problem there."

What she was about to say was the hardest thing she'd ever said to anyone. She was no actress, but she summoned every ounce of her being to appear unworried. "No problem with social media. Problem with you and me."

She saw Cory pale a little bit and reassured him. "No sweat, I mean it. Look. I can see what's happening with us. We've got this big history. And we were a couple once. But I can see that you don't want to be a couple again. But you're too much of a gentleman to come to me and say something that would hurt me. Like, what guy would do that? And I want you to know that I'm fine with that. I really am. Because I've met someone else, and I really like him. So don't worry if you don't want to be with me. You can be with anyone you want or with no one at all. Zoey, Chalice, even Kaylee Ryan if you want. It doesn't matter to me." She smiled her best smile. "See? I'm fine."

Cory looked at her closely. "You're fine?"

Alana nodded. "Totally fine. You know Ellison, right?"

"The guy in the gym?"

120

"Yep. The same. The guy we ran into in the warehouse casino with Kaylee. Well, he and I—I don't know, it's still early—we really like each other a lot. Kaylee saw us this morning."

He raised an eyebrow. "Saw you? Where?"

"I've been working out with him in the mornings. He's my trainer. And, well, she saw him kiss me."

Alana waited, trying to gauge Cory's reaction to that. He was impassive. Neither smiling nor concerned, neither jealous nor relieved. All he said, in fact, was, "Okay."

"Okay?"

"What do you want me to say, Alana? We had a great thing when we had it. And who knows what the future will bring. This isn't our time. I know it, and I think you know it. There's a lot going on with me. I'm still pretty fragile after the last year. So if you're with someone else you like and care about? I think that's great."

Huh. That was interesting; his saying that he was still fragile. Maybe it meant that he didn't think he could be with anyone at all. It made Alana feel better. Less rejected. Less like Cory was not being with her so that he could be with someone else. Someone like Kaylee.

She had to find out for herself. "Kaylee said you guys were, um, hanging out."

"We are."

She breathed in sharply. "What does 'hanging out' mean?"

Cory answered her directly. "Hanging out means hanging out. I like her. She likes me. We're starting to get to know each other. That's all."

"So, it won't get romantic?"

"I don't know. I'm not a fortune-teller. But are we rushing into anything? No," he said.

She'd gotten the answer she was looking for. He and Kaylee were not an official couple. Which meant that the door was still open for her. If it wasn't wholly open, at least it wasn't shut completely.

Then, unfortunately, he added something that stung. "I really like her, though. And I feel a lot better knowing that you and this Ellison guy are together. I didn't—I don't—want to do anything to hurt you. It wouldn't hurt you if Kaylee and I got closer, would it?"

Alana's best smile got even better. She lied through her grin in a way that would have made her father proud. "Hurt me? I think it would be great!"

Cory beamed. "That's excellent. You and Ellison are going to the wedding together?"

"We'll be at the reception together. But I can't sit with him. I'm sitting with my dad and Roxanne."

"Good luck with him."

WEDDING BELL BLUES

"Thanks," she answered with total insincerity. "So, I've got some other stuff to do. All good over there in social media?"

Cory spent a few minutes outlining what was happening in his department, hugged Alana, then left.

When he was gone, Alana sagged in her chair, too overwhelmed to cry. Cory had confirmed it. It was not Kaylee's imagination. She had brought into his life the girl who was going to steal him away from her.

She had to talk to someone who would understand. Zoey. Zoey would get it.

A couple of texts later, she and her bestie were meeting by the lifeguard stand on the pool deck. Teen Tower was open, and the usual festivities were in full swing. Kids were swimming, diving, and using the water-park features. More were streaming in by the minute. Alana had recently instituted waiter and waitress service at the pool for non-alcoholic drinks, and servers in Teen Tower uniforms were circulating with plastic cups full of no-booze margaritas and mudslides.

"I just talked to Cory," she told Zoey.

"And?"

"He likes Kaylee."

"You gotta be kidding."

Alana shook her head. "I'm not kidding. I told him I'm

hanging with Ellison these days, and he didn't care. He was *happy* for me."

Zoey took Alana in her arms. "You're hanging out with Ellison? Are you kidding? Good for you! He certainly is eye candy. But it sucks that Cory was happy and not jealous. He's an idiot. That blonde twit from Texas—how dare she move in on your man."

"Cory doesn't want me, Zoey. Don't you get it? He doesn't want me."

Zoey stepped away and looked at her. "No tears. You hear me? No one sees you crying."

Alana nodded. "Okay."

"Here's the thing," Zoey told her. "You've got the power here. You hired Kaylee, you can fire Kaylee. You can run her out of town if you want. It would be easy."

"That's not the answer," Alana said sadly. "It wouldn't make Cory like me more. In fact, he'd like me less if he found out I'd done it."

Zoey laughed. "But tell me it wouldn't make you feel better. Go on. Tell me that."

Alana didn't answer. She wasn't sure that firing Kaylee would make her feel better. But she wasn't sure that it wouldn't *not* make her feel better either.

"Ah. You're thinking about it."

Alana nodded. "Yeah."

124

WEDDING BELL BLUES

"Keep doing that. While we're on the subject of thinking … have you thought about a wedding gift for your dad and Roxanne?"

"Yeah. A little." She had thought about it, especially after Roxanne had presented her with that gorgeous bracelet the day before. But she had no idea what to get them. What did a person buy for a couple that had everything there was in the world to have?

"And you decided on …?" Zoey prompted.

"I don't know," Alana admitted. "I've been a little distracted."

Zoey put an arm around her shoulder and started walking her away from the lifeguard stand toward the game room. "Listen. Let me handle it for you. I'll pick it, wrap it, write your card, everything. All you have to do is sign it."

"You would do that?"

"Sure. And because it's me doing it, you know it's going to be great," Zoey assured her.

"Deal," Alana told her.

There wasn't another person in the world whom she'd let do what she'd just decided to let Zoey do. She knew Zoey would not let her down. And that thought, on a day that had started out bad and gotten worse, made her feel at least a little better.

125

CHAPTER THIRTEEN

The wedding rehearsal dinner was to be at Mondrian. It was a small affair in comparison to the massive wedding party of the next day. As Alana dressed for dinner, she thought through tomorrow's program. There was actually no need for this rehearsal because the wedding itself would be the simplest thing in the world. It was scheduled for two in the afternoon in the rotunda of the county courthouse; the governor would officiate. There would be just a few attendees. Roxanne's mother and father were coming from the East Coast, along with a younger sister still in college. Also, Steve's younger brother, David, who lived in France. She herself, of course. Other than that and the happy couple, just an official photographer.

The reception, though, would be a different story.

When all the RSVPs came in, and the heads were counted, fifteen hundred people were expected in the Desert Ballroom for a black tie affair that would be as much like a variety and awards show as a wedding party. It seemed like every major act performing in Vegas that weekend would be putting in an appearance. Celine Dion, Green Day, Penn and Teller, Garth Brooks, Sting, Ziggy Marley, Kanye, Beyoncé … the list went on and on.

There would be a dance floor, but seating would be like at an awards banquet. There would be rotating masters of ceremonies, from Louis C.K. to Chris Rock to Jay Z to Ellen DeGeneres. That Steve could attract this talent on such short notice was a testament to his own star power. Even Alana was impressed.

Both Zoey and Chalice had insisted on helping Alana get ready for the rehearsal dinner. They'd gotten her into one of the two sleeveless dresses she'd be wearing that weekend. This one was ochre, by Zac Posen, and it showed off her newly toned triceps to great advantage. Her Narciso Rodriguez dress for the wedding reception was a one-shouldered black chiffon confection that was both demure and sexy. She looked great in both, having lost all six pounds she'd wanted to lose in record time. When her friends asked her how she did it, she confessed that she'd been training in the mornings with Ellison.

"You need to keep training," Zoey told her after they'd zipped up the dress.

"Can you ask Ellison if he could train us too?" Chalice asked.

Zoey shook her head darkly. "Would that 'us' include your new best friend, Kaylee Ryan?"

"Kaylee's nice," Chalice protested. "You should hang out with her sometime."

"No way," Zoey sniffed. "Not after she poached Cory."

"It's okay," Alana told them both. "I know Cory's into her. And it's fine. I told her so, and I told him so. I'm going to the wedding with Ellison."

Her friends stared at her. "You're kidding," Zoey said flatly. "I can't believe you're fine with it. I know Ellison is a distraction for you, but stop pretending you're over Cory."

Alana shook her head. "Nope, I'm serious. It's all good."

Zoey spun around toward Chalice. "Did you know that your New Best Friend and Cory are a couple?"

Chalice grimaced. "Well … kinda sorta a little."

"You could have warned Alana, you know," Zoey hissed.

"It's okay, Zoey," Alana said. She noticed Zoey's angry glare at Chalice. She didn't want a big mess between her

two old friends. Not tonight. Not on the wedding weekend. It would just be too painful.

"No," Zoey disagreed. "It's actually not okay." She edged toward Chalice, her blue eyes glinting dangerously. "You know, I think you need to decide whose team you're on. You can be on Alana's team, or you can be on Kaylee's team. But you can't be on both teams. Understand?"

Chalice held her ground. "I had nothing to do with Cory and Kaylee getting together. I'm just saying that I think she's a nice person. And she's been nice to me. Maybe you should get to know her."

Zoey shook her head. "I know her enough already. And now I know she poached the guy that the person who's *supposed* to be our best friend likes."

"That's not fair. I told her it was fine," Alana cautioned. She went to her shoe closet for her shoes, a pair of sexy black Manolos.

"So what?" Zoey asked.

"So what, what?"

"So what if you said that to her!" Zoey exclaimed. "It doesn't matter what you said. She shouldn't have done it." She snapped her fingers. "Hey! I know. I could tell Cory to stay away from Kaylee."

"I don't think that's a great idea," Chalice declared.

"Me either," Alana said quietly.

"You're both wrong," Zoey said. "Alana? You've got a lot of power here. You need to learn from your dad. He'd use it. So should you." Then she shifted her attention to Chalice. "Chalice, baby? You're digging yourself right out of my heart. And if I hear that you've shared one word of this conversation with your New Best Friend, I will mess you up, and then I will mess up your family. Alana wants you to keep your redheaded mouth shut. Right, Alana?"

Alana was silent for a moment. She closed her eyes, and once again imagined her own wedding in the French countryside. This time, the groom came down the stairs toward her. He looked like Cory.

Ouch.

She nodded wordlessly to Zoey.

"Okay?" Zoey asked Chalice.

It took several long moments before Chalice said okay.

Alana put on the Manolos. No matter whether Zoey was right or wrong about Cory and Kaylee, it was heartening how loyal she was, and how helpful she'd been over the last week. Zoey had even followed through and bought the perfect wedding present for Steve and Roxanne—a set of the original keys from the Hoshi Ryokan Hotel in Japan. It was the world's oldest continually operated hotel. The keys were from the tenth century. Zoey had boasted that

it had taken all of her online shopping skills to find them. Then, she had the keys encased in a Lucite box, along with a certificate of authenticity in both English and Japanese, and wrapped it all in gold wrapping paper. Alana was sure that her dad and Roxanne would love the gift.

Zoey deserved a reward for all of this, Alana decided. Not only that, but Alana knew what the reward could be. She was on the verge of sharing her decision when there was a discreet knock at her bedroom door.

"Come in, it's safe!" she called.

It was Mr. Clermont. "Two things," he intoned. "Thirty minutes until you're due at Mondrian. And Miss Kaylee is here to see you. She says it's important."

Kaylee? Why was *she* here?

Alana stood. "Show her in, Mr. Clermont."

"Keep your mouth shut," Zoey growled at Chalice.

A moment later, Mr. Clermont ushered Kaylee through the door. She wore jeans and a T-shirt and looked tired. Chalice said hi. Zoey didn't.

"Great dress," Kaylee told Alana.

"I'm glad you're here. I need to talk to you."

"That's why I came too," Kaylee told her. "Can we step outside?"

"Hey, you're with friends," Zoey called out sarcastically.

Alana nodded to Kaylee; they stepped into the corridor leading to Alana's room. Alana closed the door behind her. "I don't have a lot of time. What's up?" she asked.

"It's about my aunt."

"She's in the hospital, right?"

Kaylee nodded. "Yep. But she isn't in the hospital anymore. She left Vegas. And she said it was *my fault*." Kaylee got choked up. Alana stood there uncomfortably.

"What happened?"

Kaylee spun a long story of how she'd said all these harsh things to Karen while she was asleep in her hospital bed, but it turned out that Karen had actually heard them. "I was mean," she concluded. "I was horrible. I told her she couldn't ruin my life anymore."

Alana pursed her lips. "That doesn't sound mean. That sounds honest."

"I guess," Kaylee murmured, tears sliding down her face. "But it still hurts."

Kaylee looked so sad and forlorn that Alana embraced her gingerly. She had such mixed feelings about Kaylee, but she knew the pain of losing a relative, even when that relative was acting crazy. Kaylee had to be having that same experience. No one deserved that.

"Okay," Kaylee said after the short hug. "I know you've got the dinner. I just wanted to tell you in person.

WEDDING BELL BLUES

I won't have to miss any more work because of Karen. Sorry to bother you."

"It's fine," Alana assured her.

Kaylee shook her head. "Actually, it isn't fine. But it is what it is. Have fun tonight. I'll see you at the party tomorrow. And you really do look great. What did you want to talk to me about?"

Alana shook her head. Time was getting tight. "It can wait."

She bid Kaylee good-bye and watched her assistant walk away. When she'd heard Mr. Clermont's announcement that Kaylee was there, she thought it might be a fated time to tell all three of her friends about the decision she'd made regarding Zoey. But with Kaylee so upset, that would seem like piling on. However, that didn't mean she couldn't tell Zoey and Chalice. She made a mental note to talk to her dad about the aunt's disappearance. It seemed too convenient.

"What'd the blonde vulture want?" Zoey asked after Alana returned to the room.

"Something personal."

Zoey perked up. "She's breaking up with Cory?"

"Nothing to do with Cory," Alana told them. "But I have something to say that has to do with you, Zoey."

Zoey raised her eyebrows. Chalice looked interested despite herself.

133

"I'm making a change at Teen Tower," Alana announced. "You're my new exec assistant. Co-assistant, that is. Don't mention it to Kaylee yet, though. I'll do that myself."

Chalice audibly sucked in her breath, and Zoey looked momentarily stunned. Then she narrowed her eyes and smiled.

CHAPTER FOURTEEN

The rehearsal dinner was painless. There were few enough people for the whole wedding party to be comfortably seated at a table for eight. Roxanne's sister, Demetria, made a toast as the maid of honor, while Steve's brother, David, toasted the happy couple as best man.

Demetria's talk was all about Roxanne's obsession with goldfish when she was a little girl, and her wish that Roxanne would be just as obsessed with Steve's happiness. David shared a funny story about how Steve was suspended from first grade for singing a bawdy song at the top of his lungs on the school bus. He wished for his brother to make that bawdy song come true on the wedding night. Mostly, Alana chatted with Demetria, who interned at the United Nations.

The meal was a French-Japanese fusion feast. There was tuna belly meat, Japanese amberjack with nigeri, giant clams, gizzard shad, abalone, boiled sea eel, and more— twenty-five courses in all. The mood was convivial. Wine and Champagne flowed, but no one got too polluted, not even Uncle David, who was known for not being afraid of a drink.

Her dad and Roxanne seemed really happy. Alana was subdued. Part of her wanted to root for the wedding to succeed. The odds of a long, happy marriage might not have been great because of the age difference and because Steve Skye was, well, Steve Skye, but that didn't mean it wasn't worth a shot. As long as no one got pregnant, their getting married wasn't all that different from their hooking up. Alana had no doubt that Steve had made Roxanne sign a prenup agreement, so there'd be zero claim on the family fortune.

That said, it was hard for Alana to think about love when she was in such a weird place with Cory and Ellison. The guy she wanted was Cory. Ellison was there in the meantime and didn't seem to mind. But when she'd closed her eyes and imagined her own wedding at that church in the French countryside, the groom was not Ellison.

The other hard thing to reconcile was the idea of a stepmother. There was nothing that anyone could do to

WEDDING BELL BLUES

bring her mom back to sanity. She was certifiably nuts. Even so, the reality of her father's remarriage shined a big light on the hole in Alana's heart: a hole the size and shape of her mother.

Between the fresh-caught trout sushi and the rock cod sashimi, Alana graciously slipped away from the table, muttering that she needed to use the ladies' room. That was true. What wasn't true was that the ladies' room was her only destination. She walked through Mondrian, passing the happy diners and the paintings by the Dutch impressionist master. The artist Jeff Koons was working on a painting in the Mondrian studio, and she stopped for a moment to watch him apply a few brushstrokes to an enormous canvas. Then she left the restaurant and detoured to the escalator that brought her up to the hotel lobby. There she found an empty overstuffed chair behind a tall column, sat, and took out her cell.

She found the number she'd called a few days before and pressed it to redial. A moment later, she was connected to her mother's mental health facility in Georgia. It was a long shot, she knew. Disappointment was the most likely outcome.

"Hello," she told the receptionist. "I'm Alana Skye, and I'm on Carli Warshaw's call list. May I speak with my mother, please? Is she still awake?"

After the usual challenge-code thing, the receptionist asked Alana to hold. "Stand by. This could take a few minutes."

Alana bided her time by watching the usual parade of people through the LV Skye lobby. It was a mix of people from all over the world. At this hour, those checking in looked tired after a day of traveling. Otherwise, the lobby was full of happy folks on their way to dinner, to shows, or to the casino.

"Alana?"

Alana froze. Her heart skipped a beat. It was her mother.

"Mom?"

"Yes." Carli's voice was measured and calm. "It's your mother. Hi, sweetie. I'm glad you called. It's been a long time."

"Yes, it has." Alana tried to calm herself. She failed. "You know I tried to call you before. Earlier this week."

"I know, sweetie. And I'm sorry I didn't ring you back. It's hard for me. But I got the message that you called. And it means a lot that you're even thinking about your mom. How's my daughter? Eighteen now, right? Happy birthday!"

Alana got choked up. Her mother hadn't called or sent anything to wish her a happy birthday a few weeks

ago. She hadn't felt bad because she'd learned to expect nothing from Carli. That her mom was remembering now meant she hadn't been forgotten. Not only that, she sounded lucid. It wasn't impossible for her to sound lucid, but it was rare.

"I'm good, Mom," Alana managed to say. "And how are you?"

"Good, good."

There was so much to say, and so much that Alana couldn't say. There wasn't much time; she had to get back to the rehearsal dinner. Why had her mother picked this time to come to the phone instead of another?

"Mom, listen. I have to get back to something in a minute. But there was something I wanted to ask you. Need to ask you, really," Alana told her.

"What, sweetie?"

"I'll call you again, I promise," Alana rushed on.

"I know you will. What did you want to talk to me about?"

Alana breathed in, then out. She didn't want to shock her mother, but …

"Listen. The thing I have to get back to? It's the rehearsal dinner for Dad's wedding. He's getting remarried tomorrow, and—"

"I know," her mother interrupted.

She couldn't believe what her mother had just said.

"Excuse me?"

"I know, Alana," her mother said softly. "Dad called me about a week ago. Said he was happy, and that this was a good woman. She sounds young to me, but I don't know. I told him it was okay with me."

"He called you?" Alana's mind reeled. "He didn't tell me that."

"Did you ask him?" Carli asked pointedly.

"No, but—"

"Maybe you guys need to work on your communication skills. Anyway, it's fine with me that he's remarrying. It doesn't affect you and me. You have a mother, and it's me. I will always be your mom."

Alana's cell sounded with an incoming text. It was from her dad.

"Where are you?"

"Mom?"

"Yes?"

"I've got to go. They're wondering where I am."

"Then go," Carli told her. "Have as much fun tomorrow as you can. Your dad says it's going to be quite the bash."

"Okay, Mom." Alana marveled at how good her mother was sounding.

Carli cleared her throat. "And one more thing."

"Yeah, Mom?"

"When it comes time for your own wedding? I'll be there. I promise," Carli declared.

That choked Alana up all over again.

"Bye, Alana," Carli told her. "I love you."

"Bye, Mom. I love you too."

Alana hung up. She looked around the lobby. It sparkled through the tears that glistened in her eyes like diamonds from her soul.

CHAPTER FIFTEEN

Dad?"

"Yeah?"

"Can I ask you something?"

Alana stood with her dad together in the rotunda of the county courthouse. On this Saturday morning, the courthouse was closed. Steve had arranged for the building to be opened for the purposes of his wedding. The governor was due to arrive in ten minutes.

Roxanne was in one of the courtrooms adjoining the rotunda, having a few private moments with her mother and sister while she adjusted her dainty Chanel suit; she'd save the stunning Vera Wang creation for the extravagant reception. Alana's uncle was in the men's room fussing with his Prada tie. For the first time in a long time, Alana

was alone with her dad. She wore a tea-length Dior dress; he was in an elegant Ralph Lauren gray suit.

"Sure, of course. What can I help you with?"

For once in Alana's life, Steve sounded like a real father, not a person trying to teach her a lesson about how to succeed in the hotel business, or getting her to be the kind of daughter he wanted her to be. She thought she should take advantage of it while it lasted.

"What would you think if I told you that I called Mom?"

Steve got the strangest look on his face. A mixture of shock, relief, and also admiration. "Did you?"

Alana nodded. "Yes. A few times."

"Did she talk to you?"

She nodded again. "Not at first. But she came to the phone last night. She sounded … I don't know … sane."

"Don't let that fool you. I get reports from the psychiatrists every month," her father declared. "She's as bipolar as they come. You just happened to catch her in the middle of her cycle. Good timing. It must have felt good, though."

"It was," Alana acknowledged. "It was comforting."

"Did you talk about the wedding?"

"Dad, that's why I called her. I didn't realize you'd already told her."

"I'm glad you got to talk to your mother."

Her breath caught in her chest. "Why didn't you tell me that you called her? That you told her you were getting remarried," Alana asked him.

Her father scratched his chin. "Hold it. Didn't we just celebrate a birthday for you?"

"Sure, yeah."

"Eighteenth as I recall," Steve said vaguely.

"Yes."

"Well, like Roxanne told you about being in the wedding, you're an adult like we are. If I call your mother and decide to tell you, I will. If you call her and decide to tell me, you will. Otherwise," Steve concluded, "I'd say it's none of each other's business, no?"

Then he softened. "I have to say, Alana. I'm glad you spoke to her. Carli's your mother. She's always going to be your mother. No one can ever replace her. Not in here …" He touched Alana above her heart. "Or in here." He touched his own heart and then continued. "Life goes on. You can meet someone else. You can fall in love with someone else. But you can't replace a person with another person. They can live in your heart side by side, but one doesn't take the place of the other."

Alana thought about herself, Cory, and Ellison. Her father was right. Ellison was not taking the place of Cory in her life. But Cory didn't love her. Ellison might, someday.

144

WEDDING BELL BLUES

But for that to happen, Alana had to make room for him and tell him that the room was there. It would be weird, though, having Ellison side by side in her heart with a boy who didn't love her, a boy who didn't really want to be there at all. Cory was in her heart, for sure. But she wasn't in his. She pursed her lips. It wasn't fair. It *so* was not fair.

"You okay?" her father asked.

She nodded. No way was she going to wreck her dad's wedding with her own feelings. That, above all, would not be fair.

"I'm good," she told him. "You look great. Let's have a wedding."

"Let's have a wedding indeed!"

A politician's practiced voice boomed as the governor of Nevada came bounding down the stairs from the second floor of the courthouse. He'd obviously come in through a separate entrance. Then Roxanne, her mother, and sister all came into the rotunda.

The bride and groom were there. The governor, the families, and even the child of the groom was there. The only person missing, Alana thought sadly, was Cory.

When Alana closed her eyes and thought about her own wedding someday in the future, she never got further than the ceremony at the small church in the French countryside.

145

She didn't spend a moment on the wedding reception. Yet as she stepped into the Desert Ballroom of the LV Skye, wearing the Rodriguez cocktail dress and carrying a silver clutch bag, Alana knew that her own party wouldn't look anything like this over-the-top circus of fame and money.

The Desert Ballroom was the largest hall at the hotel. It was used for big awards shows and convention meetings and dinners. For the reception, it had been done up in the party's black-and-white theme. The walls were so well draped in those colors that it was impossible to know what was behind them.

There were more than a hundred round-top tables arranged around the room. The head table was closest to a stage that featured a dance band that played as guests arrived. There were ice sculptures, a black-and-white art gallery, and even a small hall of black-and-white photographs from some of the most famous photographers in history. Black-clad waiters and waitresses circulated with cocktails and Champagne as the fifteen hundred guests filed in past security.

The only person who wasn't wearing black, white, or some combination thereof was Roxanne. She'd made a grand entrance in her fuchsia wedding gown. It was an amazing concoction of tulle and silk, and it clung in all the right places. It made her easy to pick out.

WEDDING BELL BLUES

"You look beautiful," Roxanne told Alana.

"You too," Alana said sincerely. "Marriage agrees with you."

"For the moment. Talk to me in thirty days," Roxanne said slyly. She nodded in the general direction of Alana's left wrist. "The bracelet … it's gorgeous."

Alana grinned. It was so much easier to talk with Roxanne now that she'd had that conversation with her mother. And that talk with her father in the rotunda of the courthouse. If both her dad and Roxanne were going to treat her as an actual adult, it might be possible for the three of them to maybe coexist in the same penthouse. Maybe.

"I know. Thank you," Alana told her.

"Okay. I'm going to circulate," Roxanne said. "Have fun tonight, okay?"

"I'll do my best," Alana promised.

She gave it a good effort. Sitting at the head table, she didn't get to hang out much with her own friends or even Ellison. Again, she talked mostly with Roxanne's sister, and a little with her uncle. There were rotating masters of ceremonies; she laughed until her stomach hurt at Louis C.K.'s comments about how scared he would have been to date Steve Skye. And Ellen DeGeneres's imitation of her father playing guitar with ZZ Top was hysterical. She

147

loved the performances from Sting, Rihanna, and Ziggy Marley. And the food was to-die-for—better even than when Jean-Claude Chanderot had presented it for the first time in Haiku.

She laughed. She smiled. She greeted the hundreds of people who stopped by the head table to offer congratulations to her dad and Roxanne. Many of them took a moment to congratulate Alana on the success of Teen Tower. It felt great, but it also felt a little dishonest. She knew that the success wasn't her success. If it hadn't been for Kaylee and her great ideas in those days right before the Teen Tower opening, her father would have never given control of the project back to her. She would have been humiliated.

It was killing her that Zoey and Chalice knew that Zoey was being promoted. Kaylee was going to have to work with Zoey, but Kaylee didn't know. Yet. Holding the secret was the kind of thing that didn't bother her father, but it bothered Alana a great deal. The wedding seemed like a crazy time to share the news. She knew Zoey's feelings about Kaylee. At some point, it would be impossible for her friend to keep her mouth shut. There would be too much pleasure in lording it over Kaylee. But if Kaylee felt at all bad about the Zoey thing, she ought to be happy to hear how Steve was helping to protect her from her aunt.

The only thing holding Alana back from talking to Kaylee right then and there was Cory. All through the meal, she scanned the ballroom to see if he and Kaylee were together in any way that could be seen as more than just "friends." They had, in fact, been seated at the same table, along with Ellison, Zoey, Chalice, and a bunch of other people whom Alana knew from high school. What was good was that every time Alana glanced in their direction, Kaylee and Cory were talking to other people. They weren't even sitting next to each other.

That fact made Alana confident enough to want to talk to Kaylee about the Zoey thing. Wedding reception or no wedding reception.

When Kanye finished his first song, but before he started his second, Alana got to her feet and told her dad that she was going to say hi to her buds. He was too distracted by well-wishers to acknowledge her comment. Alana grabbed her phone from her clutch. Then she drifted away from the head table. She thumbed in a quick text to Kaylee.

"Hi. Meet me by Champagne fountain."

A moment later, a text sounded from her friend.

"U gonna push me in again?"

Alana laughed so loudly that people around her stopped what they were doing to look. She and Kaylee had

149

met at Alana's birthday party, where Kaylee was helping serve drinks and appetizers. Some drunk guy clumsily knocked into Alana, and Kaylee got between Alana and the party's Champagne fountain. Ultimately, Kaylee took a "bubble" bath. Alana brought her up to the penthouse to let her shower and borrow one of her dresses, and the rest was history. Good history, Alana realized. All except for the Cory thing. Whatever that thing was.

She thumbed back one more text to Kaylee.

"Ha! Just meet me."

Alana made her way to the fountain, which was in the rear left corner of the giant ballroom. Kanye started another tune, and everyone stayed seated to listen to him, which made traversing the ballroom a snap.

And there she was. Kaylee looked beautiful. She wore a BCBG black lace dress, strappy black sandals, and carried a black patent-leather clutch. She'd curled her blonde hair and had on the barest amount of blush and lipstick. When she approached, Alana spontaneously grabbed two water-filled crystal goblets from a passing waiter.

"How about a toast to the happy couple?"

Kaylee took a goblet and raised it. "To you and Ellison?"

Alana laughed and covered any discomfort. "That's not what I had in mind, but sure. Why not?"

They drank.

"I can't stay long, but there's something I want you to know," Alana shared.

Kaylee peered at her knowingly. "About Zoey being your assistant too? She already told me."

Damn that Zoey. Alana was pissed. She couldn't even keep her mouth shut for twenty-six hours. This was not a good way to build their professional relationship. In fact, it was a pretty crappy way. Alana, though, had learned at least one thing from her father. The angrier he got in a business setting, the more controlled he appeared to be.

Alana raised her eyebrows. "Really?"

"No, Alana. I'm making it up. Of course really."

Alana sighed. "I deserved that. Okay. I'm sorry. You should have heard it from me first."

"It's true?"

"Yeah, it's true. She's been great this week. I think I could really use two assistants. It'll be fine."

She paused for a moment, thinking of what else she wanted to say. This was much harder than she'd thought it would be. Her feelings about Kaylee were more mixed up than ever. Then she remembered the other thing she wanted to talk about, but Kaylee broke in before she could get another word out.

"Hey. It's your call. But I'm telling you—if she treats

me badly? There's only so much I can take. If it's too much, I'm out of here. Nothing is worth being abused for," Kaylee said.

"Duly noted."

"I mean it. And you'll miss me."

"Relax, Kaylee," Alana told her. "It'll be fine."

It would be fine, Alana thought. Because if she heard about Zoey abusing Kaylee, it would be Zoey who would be fired, not Kaylee.

"It's going to snow tomorrow too."

Both girls laughed. For a moment, it felt like old times. B.K.C. Before Kaylee and Cory.

Kaylee drank some of her water, then put down the glass. "Is that all you wanted to tell me? Because this is kind of a weird time."

"No. There's something else. It's about your aunt. I found out why she left town."

"Oh?"

"And I can predict with full confidence that she'll never come back. It isn't in her best interest to come back. Staying as far away from Vegas as possible is what will benefit her the most." Alana smiled mysteriously. Kaylee was about to be blown away.

Kaylee raised her eyebrows. "What's that supposed to mean?"

"It means my dad wants you to be able to do your job without worrying about her, which is pretty funny considering that you're talking about quitting. Nice dress, by the way."

"Thanks about the dress. Clueless about your dad and my aunt."

Alana looked around. She didn't want anyone to overhear what she was saying. It was no problem. Kanye had finished his set; her father was bounding up to the stage to thank him and talk to the crowd. Alana continued. "Okay. Here's the thing. He told me that he paid her to leave. And he's paying her to stay away."

"What! That's ... that's crazy!"

Just as Alana expected, Kaylee was floored by this news. Steve was investing in her. What Kaylee didn't know was that Steve was a very careful investor. In the medium-term and the long-term, it would very much be in Kaylee's best interest to stay at the LV Skye, no matter what abuse Zoey brought down on her.

"Nope. It's just my dad. And ... holy—look at that!"

The lights on the stage changed; a spotlight focused on her father. And then, behind him on a scrim, a red wash of color gave way to backdrop art of a man in a mask. Alana recognized the mask right away. So did much of the audience, and so did Kaylee, whose hands flew to her mouth

in surprise. In case anyone didn't recognize the mask, the word "PHANTOM" appeared against the mask in big block letters that could be read by every guest.

Steve raised the mic to his mouth. "Ladies and gentlemen! For your entertainment tonight, in anticipation of his new gig at Teen Tower, the LV Skye presents the hottest magician and escape artist in town, the young man the whole city is buzzing about ... Phantom!"

This was stunning. Steve hadn't told Alana that Phantom would be performing tonight. He hadn't told anyone. He was springing this as a surprise. And why not? Anyone who was anyone in Vegas was in this room. Was there any better way to announce that LV Skye had secured the services of the town's next big thing?

From the look on Kaylee's face, it was obvious that she didn't know either. Which meant that whatever negotiations had been done between Steve and Reavis had been done in secret.

Huh. They'd both kept their mouths shut. Impressive.

Reavis appeared on the stage accompanied by a new assistant—a young woman in her twenties who looked vaguely North African. With her help, he ran through a gamut of tricks. He sliced the woman into four parts in a box and put her back together. He made a pitcher of water freeze in mid-pour just before the water hit the floor.

154

WEDDING BELL BLUES

His final routine was a levitation act where he somehow raised himself up and over the audience. This last one got a standing ovation.

"Did you know anything about this?" Kaylee asked as Reavis floated above their heads.

"Like you said before, clueless."

When Phantom's act was over, the band started playing. It was a mellow jazz number. As Alana watched, Roxanne joined Steve on the stage. The audience applauded enthusiastically.

"Come on," she encouraged the crowd. "Come and dance with us."

Alana saw her go into her father's arms. He was a good dancer; she was passable. He waltzed her around the stage as dozens, then scores, then hundreds of people got up from their tables to dance in honor of the new couple.

What to do? The only thing to do would be to dance too. She would go to Ellison. Kaylee, presumably, would go to Cory. This would be the time, Alana realized. The time where Cory would see her with Ellison, realize what an idiot he'd been, and cut in to dance.

"You heard my stepmother. Shall we?" Alana asked Kaylee.

"You're the new stepdaughter, it's your call."

"Well, I want to stay on my dad's good side. Let's do it."

They headed for the dance floor. It was easy for Alana to spot Ellison. At six four, he was one of the tallest African American guests at the party. He towered over most everyone else. She was glad to see that he was scanning the crowd, looking for her. She waved, feeling a little shy in the moment. He beamed at her and offered her his arm. She took it.

She should have known it. Ellison was a sensational dancer. He moved her body against his like he was the music itself. He was so good, in fact, that others cleared space for him to operate. Alana found herself the center of attention as the band shifted to what the band leader announced was a Frank Sinatra standard. That made sense, Alana thought, as Ellison shifted from a waltz to a foxtrot. Sinatra was like the patron saint of Las Vegas.

She gave herself over to the dance and to Ellison and even closed her eyes.

When she opened them, she found they were just feet from Cory and Kaylee.

This was the moment. Here it was. The moment for him to …

Cory kissed Kaylee. She stared. She couldn't help staring, even though she was in the arms of a spectacular man who looked like a Nubian god, who could dance like

WEDDING BELL BLUES

the wind, and recite whole books from memory. Every millisecond of the kiss between Cory and Kaylee felt like being stabbed in the heart.

She tried to look away. She couldn't. Not even when Cory and Kaylee broke apart, and her eyes met Kaylee's.

"You okay?" Ellison asked. "You stopped moving."

"Me?" Alana answered bravely. "I'm great. You're a great dancer."

"It's my partner," Ellison said modestly.

The music swelled. Alana felt Ellison's arms around her. They felt safe. Calming. She breathed deeply, took Ellison by the arm, and walked him to the other side of the dance floor as far from Cory and Kaylee as they could be.

He didn't protest, but he did wonder aloud. "Any reason we're moving?"

She smiled at him. "Better view. Dance with me."

He did. She prayed that the song would never, ever end. She closed her eyes and tried, for one last time, to imagine her own wedding day. She thought maybe if she tried hard enough, she could change the script. She conjured up the little church, the French countryside, the people, and her own self standing on fresh-cut grass in her sumptuous wedding gown. This time, her groom was going to come

157

outside for her. It was time for the wedding. She looked to the church door and wished for someone very tall, very dark, and very handsome.

There he was. Tall, yes. Handsome, yes.

But sandy-haired. Still Cory.

She clung to Ellison and kept on dancing.

JEFF GOTTESFELD

Jeff Gottesfeld is an award-winning writer for page, screen, and stage. His *Robinson's Hood* trilogy for Saddleback won the "IPPY" Silver Medal for multicultural fiction. He was part of the editorial team on *Juicy Central* and wrote the *Campus Confessions* series. He was Emmy-nominated for his work on the CBS daytime drama *The Young and the Restless*, and also wrote for *Smallville* and *As the World Turns*. His *Anne Frank and Me* (as himself) and *The A-List* series (as Zoey Dean) were NCSS and ALA award-winning *Los Angeles Times* and *New York Times* bestsellers. Coming soon is his first picture book, *The Tree in the Courtyard*. He was born in Manhattan, went to school in Maine, has lived in Tennessee and Utah, and now happily calls Los Angeles home. He speaks three languages and thinks all teens deserve to find the fun in great stories. Learn more at www.jeffgottesfeldwrites.com.

WANT A DIFFERENT point of view?

JUST *flip* THE BOOK!

WANT A DIFFERENT
point of view?

JUST *flip* THE BOOK!

JEFF GOTTESFELD

Jeff Gottesfeld is an award-winning writer for page, screen, and stage. His *Robinson's Hood* trilogy for Saddleback won the "IPPY" Silver Medal for multicultural fiction. He was part of the editorial team on *Juicy Central* and wrote the *Campus Confessions* series. He was Emmy-nominated for his work on the CBS daytime drama *The Young and the Restless*, and also wrote for *Smallville* and *As the World Turns*. His *Anne Frank and Me* (as himself) and *The A-List* series (as Zoey Dean) were NCSS and ALA award-winning *Los Angeles Times* and *New York Times* bestsellers. Coming soon is his first picture book, *The Tree in the Courtyard*. He was born in Manhattan, went to school in Maine, has lived in Tennessee and Utah, and now happily calls Los Angeles home. He speaks three languages and thinks all teens deserve to find the fun in great stories. Learn more at www.jeffgottesfeldwrites.com.